AFTERWIFE

LAUREN BIEL

Library of Congress Cataloging-in-Publication Data

AfterWife/Lauren Biel 1st ed.

Printed in the United States of America

Cover Design: Sugar Free Editing

Content Editing: Sugar Free Editing

Interior Design: Sugar Free Editing

For more information on this book and the author, visit: www.LaurenBiel.com

Please visit LaurenBiel.com for a full list of content warnings.

I dedicate this book to my husband, who I would hilariously haunt from the afterlife. After almost a year of sending me memes about putting this story out, the time has finally come. I know this book is not like my usual stuff, but it's a story that spoke to me all the same. With the high levels of dark humor, I relate an annoying amount to Everett. Enjoy!

PROLOGUE

Renee lowered herself into the bath. Heat enveloped her body, permeating the thin slip clinging to her skin. *I have to do this.* Her eyes closed and she took a soft, cleansing breath, steeling herself for the coming task. Sleeping pills coursed through her bloodstream in excessive amounts, lulling her into an unnaturally calm state. Faced with death, she felt comfort. She picked up a small silver razor and played with it between her fingers. The metal flashed against the overhead light, but her mind didn't try to talk her out of her plan. She'd accepted her choice, and there was no hesitation in the surety of her grasp around the razor.

Everett.

Thoughts of her husband floated to the front of her mind. She'd already done this to him once before, but she'd make sure her end was final this time. That's where the razor came into play. There would be no encore to this show. Even a toxic cocktail of drugs wasn't enough to end her life last time, and the idle time had allowed Everett to save her. She didn't *want* to be saved.

Everett, let me go.

The thoughts of her husband weren't enough to convince her to put the razor down. If anything, they encouraged her decision. She smiled as the memories of their marriage swirled through her mental haze like a movie playing through fog. When she first met him, she'd thought he was an accountant or something because he went to a strip club in a suit. She won him over with a horrifying drink special she'd concocted herself, and he'd repaid her by bringing more joy to her life than she'd ever known.

Until he couldn't anymore.

It wasn't his fault. Renee liked nice things, and Everett's job provided the means to enjoy a life filled with them. When had the nice things stopped being enough? When had her desire for designer clothes and an increasing bank account become less important than her desire for companionship?

Please forgive me. I won't ever forgive myself.

She took a deep breath as she reminded herself that all of this—all the pain to come—was her fault. Everett worked like he did because he loved her, and she'd repaid him by . . .

She closed her eyes against the tears. Was she being irrational about this? Yes, but she saw no other course of action. The secret would have to die with her in order to be at rest for good. Her death would hurt Everett, but the secret she kept in her heart would destroy him. She had to do this. For him.

Goodbye. I love you.

CHAPTER ONE

E verett came home from work and hung his coat on the hook. He dropped his briefcase on the ground after another twelve-hour day—a common occurrence over the last six months. His exhaustion manifested as irritability most nights, and his wife was taking the brunt of it. Their marriage was hardly recognizable, and it was all his fault. They were supposed to have dinner tonight at a restaurant that was near impossible to get reservations for. Their special place. Even as the clock ticked toward dinnertime, another case had come sliding across his desk. Though he hated defending the worst criminals he'd ever met, he had to work his way up the ladder. He wanted to move up to support his family, which only made him push his wife further away. It was impossible to find the balance he needed. Irritable and fatigued, he blew out a breath and brushed his hand through his light brown hair.

Renee's going to kill me.

He'd chosen to be a defense attorney because he thought he'd be helping innocent people avoid unjust convictions. In reality, most of the people who released cries of innocence were pretty fucking guilty. Cases so cut and dry that he exhausted himself trying to find some way to plant a seed of doubt in the minds of the jurors. Winning wasn't as simple as getting a not-guilty verdict. Sometimes winning was getting your client twenty-five years instead of a life sentence. But even that seemed like an insurmountable task most of the time. It was difficult to convince a group of people your client didn't deserve to be locked away eternally when he shot his wife in the chest five times and his fingerprints were on the bloody gun.

He made his way to the kitchen. Files for new clients littered the table in towering stacks of manila and white. Every time he lost another case, he tried that much harder to win the next one, inadvertently taking him away from his home and marriage until there was an unfillable emptiness between them. This deluge of shit on his kitchen table was a testament to his current situation. If they sat across from each other, his work would still place a mountain between them.

"Renee?" he called as he undid his tie. He stripped off his jacket and tossed it over the back of the couch. Silence answered him, so he called out again. "Renee! Honey?"

He walked toward the bedroom and flipped on the light, draping his tie over a hanger in the closet as he passed. An open bottle of sleeping pills caught his attention on the nightstand. He picked it up and shook it. Empty.

"We just filled this prescription yesterday," he whispered. Despite his exhaustion, an anxious realization formed in his gut and rose into his throat. This scenario was too familiar. "Renee!" he yelled louder as he sped toward the bathroom.

When he tried to turn the knob, panic wrapped a cold hand around his throat and squeezed. It was locked. He slammed his body into the door, and the wood gave way. He forced his way through and found Renee in the bathtub, surrounded by red water.

"Renee! No!" he screamed as he grabbed her under her arms and lifted her out of the bath. Her head lolled to the side, and an acrid, metallic scent rushed toward his nose. Bloody water cascaded over him and created a pinkish flood on the marble tiles. It turned his white dress shirt into a macabre tie dye pattern, but he didn't care. He couldn't care. Nothing mattered without Renee.

He laid her on the bathroom floor and touched her neck. His fingers slid along her skin, searching for a pulse as the fear of losing her blurred his vision. Her lips were softly pursed and her eyes were closed, as if she'd merely fallen asleep. A weak thrum whispered beneath his fingers. He reached for his phone, and it nearly slipped through his wet grasp. After dialing 911, he cradled it against his shoulder and held Renee closer to his chest, willing her to hold on. Fresh blood oozed from the gashes on her wrists.

"Help! My wife . . . slit her wrists in the bath. I don't know what to do!" His words were broken by weeping. He could barely comprehend the voice on the other end as he sobbed out the answers to the operator's questions. "Yes, I can feel a pulse, but it's weak."

His hands shook as he pressed her heavy, motionless body against him. He dropped the phone after giving his address, and it crashed into the puddle of water with an ominous thud. His tears fell onto her chest and blended with the droplets of water.

"Renee, why?" He knew why. Of course he fucking knew why. "It's all my fault! I'm so sorry!"

He reached over and touched her neck again, but her pulse had disappeared along with whatever hope he had of intervening. He was too late. He buried his face against her lifeless body and cried.

The phone rang, and Everett looked down as the restaurant's name came across the caller ID. He ignored the call. There was no need for reservations any longer.

CHAPTER TWO

E verett set his coffee mug on the table and dropped his head into his hands. Dark bags hung beneath his eyes because he couldn't seem to sleep without nightmares shaking him awake. He couldn't stop thinking about how Renee's thready pulse felt beneath his quivering fingers. *What if I had gotten home just half an hour earlier? What if I hit fewer red lights? What if I had waited to look over that case?* His hand brushed down his face to wipe the exhaustion away. He looked down at the card on the table.

Services for Renee Enders, April 27th, 2022, 5-7 p.m.

He looked at his watch and sighed before rising to his feet and grabbing his suit jacket from the back of the chair. He wiped at his eyes once more as he left his house and got into his car.

The drive to the funeral home was painfully silent. He missed pawing Renee's hand away as she tried to change the radio station. He'd listen to her shit music on loop if it meant he could have her back. He could still see her beside him, bopping along to a nineties boy band while she sang each word out of key. He'd rather hear that than the sound of his breath and the rumble of the engine.

He pulled into the parking lot and looked up at the large white building. He parked the car and stared straight ahead, his hands gripping the steering wheel. Today would be the last time he viewed his wife, but no matter how talented the morticians were, they would never capture her beauty. Or erase his final vision of her on the bathroom floor.

When he saw his wife's name on the door, he hesitated before opening it. It was almost surreal. It reminded him of their wedding day—the first time he saw her first name attached to his last.

Everett walked inside in a daze. Instead of finding comfort within the funeral home's interior, he felt more like he'd stepped into a hospital or an institution. The walls, furniture, floors—everything was fucking white. Everything except the black roses decorating a table in the middle of the foyer. He'd driven all over to find them. They were her favorite.

A wide hallway led toward the main room where the services would be held. He saw the corner of the casket at the front of the room. It was the lightest shade of purple, and it looked too expensive to be buried in the ground. But that's what would happen.

Someone came up behind him and touched his arm.

Everett jumped in surprise and turned. "Roman," he sighed, taking his brother into an embrace.

Roman patted his back in a gesture of comfort that felt weak. "I'm so sorry for your loss, Ev."

Everyone was sorry for the loss. He couldn't escape the phrase. He wanted to murder whoever associated that sentence with death. "Thanks. Let's go in."

The brothers approached the casket, and Everett sucked in a deep breath as Renee's face came into view. People always said the dead looked like they were sleeping, but

Everett always thought dead people just looked dead. Her cheeks held an artificial rosy glow, and they'd neglected to apply her fake lashes. Renee loved her fake lashes. Her hands rested limply over her stomach. If he turned them over, would he see the wounds she'd sliced into her tender skin?

"She's still beautiful," Roman said beside him.

His stomach turned at the hollow falsehood. Renee was most beautiful when she smiled or when the sun played through her dark hair. She was beautiful when she was alive, but not now. This thing in the casket was an empty shell. It couldn't comfort him or tease him or remind him to turn off the porch light at night.

Unable to stand another second of looking at his wife's body, Everett walked away and sat in a chair toward the front of the room, closest to the casket. Renee's parents sat behind him, her mother sobbing into a Kleenex. A stack of crumpled tissues sat beside her, as if the tears were endless. They didn't look at him, and he knew they blamed him for her death.

The funeral director took the podium and called the first speaker to come forward after giving a canned introduction. Renee's mother rose to her feet and meandered toward the microphone, stopping along the way to cast a dramatic glance into her daughter's casket. She cleared her throat before addressing the crowd.

"Renee was my last born, and I never thought she'd be the first to leave us. She loved life . . ." Her voice trailed off as Everett heard the familiar sound of someone clearing their throat beside him. He looked to the right and nearly leaped out of his skin. He shook his head, certain he was seeing a mirage or a cruel joke from God himself.

"Renee?" he whispered with his eyes wide in disbelief.

She turned to him and smiled. She was still wearing the slip he'd found her in, though she didn't have any injuries to her wrists. Thankfully. He shook his head once more and blinked his eyes. He looked back at the casket, but her body was still motionless inside.

"Did you really let them put me in that dress your mother got me?" She sucked her teeth. "It still looks awful on me."

"Renee, how?" he whispered.

Her father leaned forward and tapped his shoulder. "You could at least be quiet while her mother is speaking," he rasped.

He must have looked like he'd lost his mind. Maybe he had.

Renee rolled her eyes, stood, and crossed in front of her mother on her way to the casket. She looked down at herself in that pumpkin-orange dress and shook her head. She touched the soft black hair on the head of her body and caressed the overly painted cheeks. Placing her ghostly hands on her hips, she shot him a glare. "Honey, they did my makeup like a clown. My lipstick is all over my face! Where did you find this funeral home, anyway? Craigslist?" She sighed in disgust.

How the hell could a person judge their own funeral? How many other departed souls would be mortified by the state of their affairs, chosen by people they didn't even like?

Everett stared at her in disbelief. He looked around to see if anyone else saw her, but her mother didn't stop her speech —except to cry into the accumulating mound of tissues—and everyone else looked bored.

"Everett?" her mother said. "Everett!"

He must have looked like a deer in headlights, and the lights were actually his dead fucking wife.

"Don't you have words to say about Renee?" she said with faked pleasantry. A forced smile graced her lips.

"Yes, absolutely." He stood on a set of shaky legs and

wiped the sweat from his palms onto his pants before taking her mother's place behind the podium.

Renee walked back to Everett's seat and sat in his chair. She crossed her legs and stared at him. The pressure of ensuring he said the right thing in front of his wife at her funeral loomed over him. *Another chance to disappoint her all over again.*

He cleared his throat. "What can I say about Renee? She was my best friend and the best wife I could ask for. She stood by me as I finished school and worked hard to build our life together." His voice trembled, and a tear dropped down his cheek, splattering on the wooden stand in front of him. "She encouraged me every step of the way. I'll miss her every day until my very last breath, and I hope she knows that." He turned his face to look in her direction. "And I hope she knows I'm sorry for not being there for her when she needed me." His voice broke as he tried to choke out the last of his speech. There was so much more he wanted to say, but it would make their marriage look marred, and he didn't want to confirm what everyone else suspected.

Everett wiped his face with the back of his hand and excused himself. He stopped at the casket and looked down at the embodiment of his wife before heading back to his chair.

"I hate to say it, but you're right," he whispered from the side of his mouth when he sat beside her. "You look ridiculous. I'm failing you even in death, Renee."

"What'd you say, Everett?" Her mother touched his arm.

"Oh, nothing," he said as he tried to figure out how his wife was simultaneously in the casket and beside him—with her dark brown eyes open and awake. Maybe he was hallucinating from lack of sleep.

Renee remained seated beside him for the remainder of the service. It was hard to stop himself from laughing or acknowledging her witty commentary as family and friends stood before the room and spoke of her. When the last person climbed down from the podium, the pianist played a gentle tune as everyone stood to pay their last respects to the dead body.

"You couldn't have asked them to play some NSYNC or Backstreet Boys?" Renee asked. "God, Everett, it's like you don't even know me."

"I'm sorry. I just didn't think 'Bye, Bye, Bye' would be very appropriate, given the circumstances," he mumbled.

He took his place by the head of the casket with the ghostly Renee by his side. As people walked by, he shook their hands or hugged them, internally screaming with every palm that pressed against his. There was no way to not be rude. He was just trapped, touching near-strangers. He kept his arm hanging at his side between guests, cringing at the thought of another hand slapping onto the others, the ghosts of their germs still on his skin. It repeated over and over again until his nerves were rubbed raw and he felt like leaving his wife's funeral. Or slamming his neck beneath the heavy lid of the fancy fucking casket. Death by annoyed sorrow.

"I'm sorry for your loss," another faceless voice said.

I hope I never hear those words again after today. Sweat beaded on his forehead as he stiffly stood in his suit and repeated the same motions once more. The worst part? Most of the guests held an air of inconvenience, as if they'd rather be curating their lawns with tweezers than attending Renee Enders' funeral. Like they were only there under obligation. When he died, he wanted none of this. He'd haunt anyone who put him on display and forced people he hardly knew to come view him at his worst.

"Oh my god, it's our old neighbors! Why are they here? They hated us!" Renee shouted, startling Everett. He looked over at her. "Remember when they took pictures of us having sex? They posted them on our door with a note about how we should close the curtains. I never told you this, but I left the curtains open on purpose."

Everett laughed as he reached a hand toward their old neighbor, who seemed confused by his laughter. He probably looked like he was going crazy, and when his eyes shot back to Renee, he wondered if he was.

"You baked her cookies and tried to apologize after she called us heathens and told us we were both going to hell for our sinful premarital sex," he whispered with a smirk once the old woman walked away.

Renee's smug grin fell from her face, and she released an unamused laugh. "Please tell me that your ex-girlfriend is not really here right now." Renee sucked her cheeks in. "And is she wearing a little black dress to my funeral?"

Christine hurried over with a shuffling, high-heeled gait. Her large fake breasts bounced with every movement, jostling the silver necklace hanging between them. Renee looked down at her own chest, which she'd always felt was inadequate. Christine passed a Jesus statue with its head bowed, probably looking at the same inappropriate cleavage Everett fought to tear his eyes away from.

"Oh, Everett, I'm so sorry for your loss!" Christine said as she wrapped her arms around him. Her chest pressed against his.

Renee leaned toward his crotch and squinted. "Really? Did you just get hard at my funeral?" She rolled her eyes.

Everett pulled away from Christine and covered his crotch with the only thing within reach—a framed picture of Renee.

"And you think *that's* any better?" She folded her arms over her chest.

Everett's cheeks warmed. That was definitely low. If Jesus over there was looking, he'd be mortified.

"She was so much more beautiful in person. Pictures don't do her justice," Christine said as she reached for the picture.

Before she could grab it, Everett tilted it away from her hands and moved his hips with it to keep his erection hidden from view. "Yep, she was. My sweet . . . sweet Renee."

Christine offered a confused nod and moved on.

"Yeah, keep walking, hussy," Renee said under her breath.

Everett tensed as Roman walked toward him and embraced him with a frown plastered on his face. His forehead pressed against Everett's. His *sweaty* forehead. He leaned away from his brother and took a step out of his muscular arms. They bulged beneath the short sleeves of the navy-blue polo shirt he must have bought in the section designated for children.

Christine stood off to the side, eyeing Roman the way a starving man eyed the butcher shop window. Even Renee's lips twitched for a moment, making Everett's stomach drop. He hated that everyone—including his own wife—found his brother attractive. Shit, even *he* found his brother attractive. And it wasn't just his appearance. Everett hadn't exactly drawn the short stick in the looks department, but Roman had a suave air about him that he could never match.

"He couldn't have worn something that covers all those arm tattoos?" Renee frowned. "This is a classy fucking establishment." She threw her hands up, gesturing around the painfully poor choice of a funeral home.

"She sure was something else, wasn't she?" Roman said softly as he stared at her made-up form in the casket.

"I wish I had gotten home just a few minutes sooner. That case could have waited until the next day," Everett whispered.

Roman placed a hand on his shoulder, offering his comforting touch. "It's not the first time she's tried, Everett.

Sometimes there's nothing you can do to stop someone's path." He brushed his hand through his dark hair, a nervous habit both brothers shared.

"Bullshit!" Renee shouted.

Everett glanced at her curiously. "What?" he asked her.

"Huh?" Roman said in response to Everett.

"Nothing. Forget it," Renee whispered.

"Forget it." Everett sighed and rubbed his temples. He'd need to be more careful about responding to Renee when others were within earshot.

"I'm just saying, don't blame yourself, bro. There's nothing you could have done." Roman reached out and touched his arm, squeezed it, and walked past Everett and through Renee.

Everett's mom came over next and hugged him. She looked down at Renee in the casket. "Renee looks really beautiful."

"God, your mother is . . ."

"Wonderful!" Everett blurted as he looked down at the casket. "She looks wonderful."

"That's not the word I'd use," Renee said as she rolled her eyes. "You should hear what she's said about me since she's been here." She circled behind her mother-in-law. "I didn't know she thought you were settling so much by marrying me. Also, she said I looked like a carnival pumpkin, but that's equally your fault."

Everett hugged his mother. When he pulled away and looked back, Renee had disappeared.

CHAPTER THREE

E verett's drive home was confusing, frustrating, and mostly silent. His eyes were still heavy, and he didn't have the strength to shed another tear. He drove on autopilot, and he didn't remember taking the roads he'd driven. He took a deep breath as he pulled into the driveway of his home. Not *their* home. Just his home now. He cut the engine and sat for a moment before getting out of his car and walking up the driveway. Cold silence greeted him when he stepped inside. With a sigh, he flopped onto the couch, too exhausted to keep himself upright a moment longer.

"Hey."

Everett sat up and snapped his attention to his left. Renee sat on the couch beside him and lifted her legs toward her body.

Everett took a quick breath. "Jesus, Renee. Can you be . . . less . . . scary?"

"Sorry. I can only show up abruptly, apparently." She smirked.

"What are you doing here? How is this possible?" He shook his head. "I think this is all from lack of sleep. It's gotta be. You're a hallucination, a bit of undigested beef or whatever the fuck Scrooge said."

"I'm not a hallucination, Everett. I don't know why you can see me when no one else can, but it's really me." Renee released a long sigh.

He pointed toward the ceiling. "There's no one . . . over there to ask?"

"Over where?" She cocked her head and lifted her eyebrows.

"The other side or whatever. There's no like . . . manager over there? God?" he asked as he brushed his hand through his hair.

She shook her head. "Nope, no manager over there, Karen. And I definitely haven't met God. There isn't an instruction manual or a *Handbook for the Recently Deceased*, either. I know as much as you do."

Everett recalled how she'd vanished at the funeral. "Where do you go when you disappear?"

"It's a very bright room. Well, I say it's a room, but it's endless light. I just . . . exist until I'm drawn back to you. I think it happens when you think about me."

"I've been thinking about you since I found you in the bathroom." He dropped his head into his hands with a sigh. "Why did you do that? Why did you do this to me? To us?"

Renee looked down at her hands and picked at her nails. "I don't know, Everett," she whispered.

"How do you not know?" He stood and paced in front of the coffee table.

"I don't remember!" she jumped to her feet and stood in front of him, just as she always had when she wanted to stop his nervous pacing. But this time, her small hands passed through his arms. He could no longer feel her touch.

"You don't remember?" Everett asked, raising his voice.

"You remember our neighbor from three years ago, but you can't recall the reason you decided to end your fucking life?"

She dropped her gaze. "I'm sorry, Everett. I just don't remember."

"Convenient."

"Everett," she whispered, "you know I can't stand it when you pace. Can't you sit down?" She moved to the couch and patted the cushion next to her.

He stopped and looked at his dead wife. "You lost the right to demand concessions when you left me," he said. "I loved you, Renee. Do you realize what this has done to me?"

He didn't wait for her reply. Instead, he stormed to the bedroom, stripped off his clothes, folded them, and climbed beneath his cold sheets. He pulled the blanket over his body and closed his eyes. Hopefully, sleep would put an end to his insanity.

WHEN EVERETT FINALLY WOKE UP, it was nighttime again. He'd slept through a full day. His tired bones and trick-playing mind needed the rest. He groaned as he turned onto his back and rested his arm over his eyes, feeling as though he could sleep until tomorrow morning. But even with sleep, the nightmare would continue. Whether he slept for eight hours or twenty, Renee was still dead. What he wouldn't give to feel her beside him one more time or to see her smiling—living—face.

He lifted his arm away and sat up with a jolt when he looked next to him. "Renee!" he shouted. She lay on her back beside him, staring at him. "What are you doing here?"

"I told you. When you think of me, it draws me to you."

She smiled as she turned onto her side and tucked her arm beneath her head.

"I had hoped this was all a hallucination from lack of sleep, but here I am, refreshed and lying next to my dead wife," he said as he rubbed his temple. She caught his gaze and looked deeply into his hazel eyes. "How am I supposed to stop thinking of you, Renee? Everything here reminds me of you." He reached a hand toward her face to caress her cheek, but his fingers passed through her.

Fighting back tears, he pulled himself from the blankets. On the floor, a pair of gray sweatpants lay in a crumpled pile at his feet. He lifted them, sniffed them, and yanked them on before grabbing a black t-shirt and sliding into it.

"Have you done laundry since I died?" Renee asked as she glared at the clothes on the floor.

"Sorry, I've been a bit busy with your funeral arrangements."

"You still have to live your life. I never wanted you to mourn me like this."

Everett's head snapped in her direction. "How can you expect me to live my life when *you* were my life?"

"Your job was your life. You spent more time with your fingers shoved into a briefcase than me!"

His shoulders dropped. "So I was the reason you killed yourself."

Renee shook her head, sending her dark hair tumbling over her shoulders as she sat up. "No, that's not the reason. You can't blame yourself for my death."

"Then tell me what I can blame it on! Goddammit, Renee!"

She closed her mouth and looked away. "I don't remember."

Frustration clawed up his throat and threatened to burst from his mouth in an angry tirade. He swallowed it down. "I think you should leave now," he said with an icy edge to his voice.

She frowned, then dissipated, leaving no imprint where she once lay.

His empty stomach gurgled and turned. He hadn't eaten much of anything since her death. Preparing a meal felt too daunting for him, so he'd been surviving on saltine crackers and a block of sharp cheddar. He needed something more substantial.

Drawers opened one by one as he tried to find something to eat in the kitchen. He pulled out a jar of spaghetti sauce and some pasta before filling a pot with water and placing it on the stove. When the water began to churn and bubble, he opened the box of pasta and poured its contents into the steam. Hot water splashed onto his arm.

"Fuck!" He wiped his forehead with a shaking hand.

Staring blankly ahead, he stirred the pasta, his mind elsewhere as his body went through the motions on autopilot. He turned off the water, drained the noodles, and returned the pot to the stove. The sauce poured from the jar and coated the noodles. He dipped his spoon into the mixture and brought it up to his mouth, smacking his lips together as he tried to figure out what it was missing.

My wife, that's what it's missing. He opened the cabinet and stared at the rows of spices. *Why are there so many fucking options?*

"Add Italian seasoning, sugar, and parmesan cheese, Everett," Renee said from behind him.

He jumped backward and nearly knocked the pan of spaghetti off the stove. "Jesus H. Christ, Renee. What?"

"You must have been thinking of what I would put in the sauce if I were making it, so here I am. Italian seasoning, sugar, and parmesan cheese." She pointed toward the cabinet and fridge.

He turned back to the cabinet and plucked the bottles out one by one, searching for the Italian mixture. When he finally found it—in the very back of the cabinet—he twisted off the lid and shook it. Scents of sage, oregano, thyme, and garlic wafted toward him, making his mouth water. He shook the mixture over the sauce twice and pulled his hand away.

"A little more," Renee said. "You like it with a lot of flavor."

He tipped it over the pot again and shook it a few more times before stirring it.

"The sugar's in the glass container by the coffee maker," Renee said, pointing.

"I know where the sugar is. Unlike the spices, there aren't fifty fucking types of sugar to choose from." He grabbed the glass container and spooned in some sugar. Lastly, he pulled the finely shredded parmesan cheese from the fridge and sprinkled it on top. After stirring it once more, he brought the spoon back to his lips, but it still didn't taste like Renee's sauce. His heart ached for that flavor. For the normalcy of a spaghetti fucking dinner.

"How am I going to do this without you?" he whispered as he set his plate on the table.

"You will, Everett. I know you will. You're the most resilient person I've ever met."

He twirled the noodles around his fork and stared at them. "Doesn't it hurt you to see me? Don't you feel the stabbing pain in your heart like I do every time I see your face?"

"More than you realize." Her hand moved toward the chair across from him—her chair—but her fingers slipped through the wood.

He got to his feet and pulled the chair out for her, just like he had on their first date. When had he stopped doing these kind things for her?

22

Her ghostly form sat in the chair, though she really just hovered slightly above it. It wasn't as unnerving when he went back to his seat since it looked almost normal from that angle.

Renee sucked in a deep breath and folded her hands in her lap. "I want to move on, but I don't know how. It would be best for both of us. The reminders of what I've lost hurt just as much as you seeing the reminder of what I took from you."

"Then we need to figure out how to help you go . . . wherever it is dead people go." He shoved a forkful of spaghetti into his mouth and forced it down. The bland glob nearly got stuck. "Because I can't live like this, and you can't die like this."

The noodles continued to catch in his throat. He stood from the table to grab a bottle of water from the fridge, but when he turned back, Renee had vanished again.

"We'll figure it out," he said to the empty room. "We have to."

CHAPTER FOUR

I t had been a few days since Everett had seen Renee, and he assumed the visions had been a culmination of grief, stress, starvation, and lack of sleep. Regardless, he was glad she wouldn't watch over his shoulder any longer, even if the silence in the house was a deafening reminder of her absence. The stillness was haunting. When he was that lonely, it was hard to stop thinking about her.

Everett turned over and looked at Renee's vacant side of the bed. He'd neglected her so much the last year. He knew that. Many nights she went to sleep alone, and even when he'd been home, he'd been too consumed with work to acknowledge her presence. Instead of thinking about her, he'd thought about how he could have presented a case better or how he could present the next case.

Taking time from work to mourn Renee gave him the freedom to appreciate her in ways he hadn't when she was alive. He sighed as he remembered tracing her curvy form with his fingertips and how her lips tasted. His dick swelled uncomfortably, and he rubbed the front of his pants. His body remembered hers so much he could almost feel what she felt like. He turned onto his back and dipped his hand beneath his sweatpants. His mind wandered to Renee, and he closed his eyes.

The salty taste of her flesh after one of her runs. Her big brown eyes as she looked up at him from her knees. The noises she made and the way her body reacted to his touch. He pulled his pants down his thighs and drew himself from his boxers. He rubbed up his length, his hand wrapped around and brushing over his excited skin. Everett let his head drop back and didn't fight the groans that wanted to leave his parted lips. His body writhed as he got closer, his thoughts so wrapped up in memories of Renee.

He recalled the first time they fucked. She'd climbed on top of him and rocked her hips until she came, shuddering against him as he clumsily thrust into her until he reached his own orgasm. The way she'd clenched around him, her come sliding down him and her breasts pressed against his chest . . .

The muscles in his abdomen tightened, and his groans became more uncontrolled and primal. As he came, he let himself call out the way he would have back when he was single and alone in his apartment, only this time, it wasn't a random cry. It was her name.

Everett rode out the pleasure before opening his eyes and reaching for something to clean up with. With a relieved sigh, he grabbed several tissues from the bedside table and rolled over. Renee's silent form was in the bed beside him, sitting up with a sly smile. He jumped up, covering his crotch with his hand.

"Jesus fucking Christ, Renee!" he screamed.

"Ev, it's nothing I haven't seen before." Her sweet smile turned flirty.

"The hell you have!" he said as he dabbed at his pelvis and wiped off his hand with red-hot cheeks.

"How haven't I?" Her grin widened further, her perfect teeth opening a bit as her tongue playfully slipped between them.

He stared at her before throwing his hands in the air. "We don't jack off quite the same way when we're by ourselves," he said. He shivered at the thought of what she'd seen. It's not that he was particularly awkward with his masturbation practices, but in his most intimate moments when he thought he was alone, he didn't watch his aesthetics. There was no holding back, and sometimes it really needed to be held back.

"I thought it was hot."

"Why are you even here, Renee?" He sighed. "It's because I thought of you, right?"

"Oh, you sure thought of me, alright." Renee's cheeks flushed and he was surprised that a spirit could feel anything that would rosy their ethereal skin.

"Now you listen to my most intimate thoughts, huh?" he asked as he pulled his pants up.

"I don't *try* to listen. Your thoughts are loudly spoken to me when I'm alone in that room. My purgatory."

"If you can appear any time I think of you, why haven't I seen you in days? You made me think I was going crazy, imagining the whole thing!" Everett's cheeks pulsed. "I know I've thought about you plenty."

"You told me it was hard for you when I was around, so I decided to give you space."

"You can choose when you come around?" With a deflated drop of his shoulders, he sat beside her on the bed.

"Kind of. But there have been times I wanted to come here when you weren't thinking of me, but I couldn't leave the room. I'm still not sure how this works."

"Renee, you're prolonging my grief by being here. I'd give anything to have you back, but not like this. It's almost worse like this because I can't touch you or smell you. You always smelled like spring."

"You think I don't want to move on as well? There has to be more to the other side than a white room. I don't know why I'm here or what I need to do to transcend, but it's something to do with you because you're the only person I can visit."

Everett scooted back and leaned against the headboard. "Don't they say spirits get stuck because of unfinished business? Is there some secret you're holding on to?"

Renee's gaze dropped for a moment before she met Everett's eyes again. "When I was supposed to get reservations at the hotel on the lake, I told you it was sold out so we wouldn't have to spend that week with your parents." She tightened her lips.

"Pretty dickish, but I don't think it's eternally damning." Everett finally let the corners of his mouth form a smirk. Renee did whatever she could to avoid the in-laws. He would do the same thing if he could.

"I put a bag of spoiled tuna in your briefcase and let you think it must have fallen out of your lunch bag and rotted," she confessed.

"What?" he said, trying to stifle a laugh. "I opened that up at a lunch meeting with the judge and prosecutor for a huge case! It stunk up the whole room! I swear that judge looked at me like I was an inept toad. Why would you do that?"

"You were being awful toward me all that week because of your fourteen-hour days at work. It was a week of projection hell. Everything I did was wrong."

Everett ran his hand through his hair. "God, I'm sorry. I definitely deserved that."

"While I'm on a roll, I also tore up your tropical shirt and said the dryer ate it." She flipped her hair over her shoulder with confidence in her decision on that one.

"Renee! The green and purple one? The one I got in Hawaii?"

"You got it in the gift shop at the airport in Hawaii. That's not the same thing. It was awful. You even wore it to a work picnic, Everett!"

"I loved that shirt," he said with true sadness over the loss of the loud shirt he loved. It was the mullet version of clothing, except it was a party from all sides.

"I was doing you a favor, I assure you." Renee crossed her legs. "Do you have anything *you* want to admit? Maybe it's something you need to tell me that's holding me back."

"Besides admitting what a shitty husband I've been?" He thought for a moment, and a pang of guilt shocked his gut. "Christine and I met for lunch six months ago. She kissed me, and I didn't stop her." He felt terrible about it. As lonely as he made Renee, he also felt the solitude of his lifestyle. Instead of trying to calm Renee's anger to get affection, it was easier to seek attention from someone who wasn't so pissed with him. But that was as far as things went. He could never be that type of husband. Neglectful? Yes. Unfaithful? No. Well . . . except for that one kiss. "It didn't go any further than that. I told her I couldn't because I love you, Renee."

"No wonder she gave you a boner at my funeral."

"That's it? No jealousy? Nothing?" Her reaction angered him. If he found out she had even so much as kissed another man, it would have driven him mad. He knew he was being a hypocrite, but he wouldn't be able to help himself.

"Of course I don't want you kissing another woman, but there's no point freaking out about it. I wasn't exactly your soft place to land after a hard day at work, so I can't blame you for wanting affection." She let out a soft laugh. "I wish I could have had these revelations when I was alive. I spent way too much of my time being bitter."

"Now I'm the one feeling angry and bitter." He dropped his gaze from hers. He was forced to carry the emotions Renee got to excuse herself from. She clocked out early and left him overwhelmed with all the work she left behind.

Renee toyed with the hem of her slip. "Well, sharing these secrets didn't help. I'm still here."

He reached for her hand, forgetting he couldn't touch her. It was easy to forget when she looked so real sometimes. So solid. He placed his hand back in his lap.

"Maybe I can't move on until I help you move on," she said with wide eyes. "Remember how I always joked that you'd better not look at another woman if I died?"

"You think your jealous threat somehow cursed us?" he said with a laugh. "I doubt that."

She turned to face him. "No, I'm serious. Maybe if we can get you back on the horse, I can leave."

That didn't sound very appealing. He didn't want to think about pursuing another woman. How would he ever find someone else who understood him the way Renee had?

EVERETT OPENED the bathroom door and saw Renee's spirit standing in the hallway. His eyes narrowed at her. "I did *not* think of you while I was in there." He pointed back to the toilet and tried to walk around her, accidentally walking through her shoulder. The temperature dropped, sending a blanket of goosebumps along his skin.

"You thought of me, even if you didn't realize it," Renee said as she followed him.

Renee stopped near the pictures on the wall. She hovered

in front of a wedding photograph. She was in her puffy white wedding dress, leaping onto Everett's back.

"Remember this picture?" she asked.

Everett touched the silver frame and ran his finger along the decorative filigree. The smiles on their faces were so perfectly timed and natural. Everything was always so natural with them. Well, it used to be. "I was still in law school then. Remember when we thought our life would finally be normal and we'd have time to enjoy being married once I finished school?" His laugh was humorless. He thought life would get better, but it went into overdrive. He never realized law school would be the easiest part. They definitely didn't teach students how to balance business and their home lives.

Renee moved to another picture. She reached toward it as if she wanted to take it off the wall to get a better look at it, but her fingers went through the frame. "Oh yeah, this was our reception. We all took a picture as a family, and your mom told me to make sure I extended my neck to prevent my double chin as the cameraman was counting down. That's why my face looks like that. I think the double chin would have been less noticeable."

"Yeah, you got so drunk after this picture that you puked all over the bathroom and made us lose our deposit. I mean, you puked on every inch of that room. You tried to tell me to take the blame, even though you were covered in vomit. Didn't take a criminal lawyer to figure that one out." Everett laughed and wished he could remain locked in the memories of his wedding day.

"I guess I did get a little sloppy, but hey, it was an open bar." She shrugged and smiled.

Everett brushed his hand through his hair and headed toward the kitchen. He poured himself a cup of coffee, grimacing as he reached for a cup for Renee. He'd never be able to have coffee with his wife again. He sat at the table, his hand still trembling around the blue mug. Steam rose and swirled inside his nose as Renee sat beside him.

"I have to go back to work on Monday," he said. He didn't feel physically or mentally capable of pretending life was back to normal, but they needed him at the office, and that always mattered more than his health.

"Are you sure you're ready for that?"

"Nope, but I have to be."

Everett brought the cup to his mouth and took a slow sip. He opened the paper from several days ago and saw Renee's face in the obituary section.

Renee Enders, 34, April 24th 2022

Renee passed unexpectedly at her home in Manlius. She was a beloved wife and daughter. Her smile could light up a room, and her laughter was contagious. Being outdoors was her favorite pastime, whether it was a jog on a winding forest trail or kayaking on the lake. She is survived by her parents, Jim and Diane Waters, and her husband, Everett Enders. In lieu of flowers, please consider a donation to your local pet shelter.

Renee leaned over to look at the newspaper. "Thank you for honoring my wish at the end. Flowers are a waste." She nodded in approval, but her lips formed a tight line when she glanced at the picture. "You chose the worst picture of me. This was from five years ago when I was at least fifty pounds heavier!"

"My mom picked it out. She thought you looked wholesome here."

"Of course she did." Renee rolled her eyes.

"Oh, shut up. You were beautiful then, and you're beautiful now." He took a deep breath, exhaling hard enough to send ripples through the coffee in his mug. "Well, you know what I mean."

"I can't see myself in mirrors or anything, but I'd like to think I look pretty good. Especially since I'm eternally stuck in this slip. I wanted to look beautiful when you found me, and you always loved it when I wore this to bed." She looked back at the obituary. "Who chose to mention my jogging? My favorite pastimes are actually sitting on the couch and binge-watching TV shows with a big ol' slice of cheesecake. And taking naps." She chuckled. "But I guess that doesn't sound as good in an obituary."

There was a knock on the door, and Everett dragged himself out of the chair to answer it. He looked back at Renee as he reached for the doorknob, putting his finger to his lips.

"I don't need to be quiet, Everett. You're the only one who can hear me."

He rolled his eyes as he opened the door. "Oh, Roman, hello."

Roman walked into the house with a pan of store-bought lasagna. *Very thoughtful.* He lifted the sunglasses shielding his dark green eyes and looked around the house as if the home had somehow changed with Renee gone. Everything was exactly how she left it, including the rescue attempts in their master bathroom. He couldn't even go in there to clean it up. Not yet, at least.

"How're you holding up, man?" Roman asked as he set the pan on the table. He looked down at the obituary. "Please tell me you haven't been staring at this," he said as he picked it up. "Not the best picture of her."

"Told you!" Renee screeched.

Everett snatched the paper from his brother and closed it. "No, I haven't been 'staring' at it. I just saw it this morning."

"Everett, I know she's your wife and this situation is horrible, but we need to go out. Get your mind off things."

Everett swallowed hard. "I'm a thirty-five-year-old lawyer, Roman. My idea of fun is winning a case with an insanity plea."

"You're pathetic." He laughed. "I don't know what she saw in you, bro."

"Everything, I saw everything in you . . ." Renee whispered, catching Everett's gaze. "Go have fun. We have to get you back on the horse, remember?"

"What did you have in mind?" Everett asked.

Roman wrapped an arm around his shoulder and stretched his arm in front of them. "Just picture it. You and me at the club, sharing drinks and checking out women like we used to."

He looked at Renee. Her eyes had glossed over, but she gave him a soft nod, urging him to say yes.

"Fine, I'll go," he said in response to them both.

Roman leaned in and shook Everett's shoulders. "The Enders brothers, back at it." Roman smiled. "I'll pick you up tonight."

"Try not to think of me, Everett," Renee whispered. "I don't think I want to see what the Enders brothers used to do."

"You're better off not knowing," Everett quipped.

"What?" Roman asked.

Everett looked away from Renee, shaking his head. "Nothing. I'll be ready."

CHAPTER FIVE

S team rose from the iron and hissed in Everett's face. He wished Renee had stuck around to walk him through ironing his dress shirt, but she'd vanished when Roman left. The last thirty minutes had been spent inserting more wrinkles into his clothes than he removed. That Hawaiian print shirt would have come in handy on a night like this. It never had wrinkles.

Everett's hip bumped into the freestanding ironing board, sending the iron tumbling off the edge. He thrust out his hands without thinking and grabbed it before it hit the ground.

"Fuck, fuck, fuck," he sputtered as the heat seared into his palm. It tumbled from his hand, defeating the purpose of grabbing it in the first place.

With gritted teeth, he rushed toward the kitchen and pushed his hand beneath the cold tap. Adrenaline surged through him, numbing the pain. He'd have to slather his hand with burn cream and wrap it before going out. Too many germs could slither into an open wound.

He stumbled toward the hall bathroom and rooted around

in the medicine cabinet. After dry swallowing three ibuprofen, he searched under the sink for the first-aid kit. *Renee always knew where this stuff was*, he thought. He waited for her to appear because he'd thought of her, but she didn't materialize. *Renee, I could really use your help right now.*

Nothing happened. He was on his own, and he'd have to search in the master bath for the kit.

The adrenaline wore off as he opened the bathroom door, and a searing pain worked its way up his arm. From fingertips to elbow, it felt as if his arm were burning from the inside out. Sweat prickled his brow, but only a small part was due to the pain. He didn't enjoy coming into this bathroom. Seeing Renee's ghost was less terrifying than the mental slideshow which played in his mind when he looked at that tub. A rust-colored stain ringed the porcelain. He'd have to hire a service to come and clean it eventually. There was no way he could stomach doing it himself.

Beneath the sink, he found the elusive first-aid kit. He pulled out the gauze pads and wrap, then opened the burn cream and slathered a thick layer over his palm. As he tucked the tail of the bandage into the haphazard wrap job, an odd smell reached his nose. Like burning plastic. He hadn't cooked anything since the disaster spaghetti, and the oven couldn't have been on that—

"Goddammit," Everett whispered.

He ran to the living room and saw lazy spirals of smoke rising from the overturned iron on the carpet. In his panic, he hadn't thought to unplug the damn thing. He snatched the cord from the wall and lifted the iron. A dark brown, triangular scorch mark adorned his beige Berber carpet.

A car horn blared outside. Everett walked into the living room and peered through the curtain. Roman's sports car waited in the driveway, outshining the energy-efficient Prius beside it. Half of him wanted to turn the lights off and pretend he wasn't home. The other half wanted to get out of the house and learn to live again. After all, it might help his wife find her way out of purgatory.

Everett slid his arms into his wrinkled shirt and flicked the light off on his way out the door.

"Hey, bro!" Roman beeped the horn, which Everett found annoying and unnecessary. He needed to tone it down several notches or there would be one more loss for people to feel sorry about.

Everett sat beside him with a groan and slammed the door. "Don't be annoying."

Roman wore a dress shirt and dress pants as well, but in a deep blue color as opposed to Everett's dark gray. Roman not only dressed better, but his jaw was more angular, and his green eyes were more striking than Everett's hazel. His arms filled out his shirt instead of sitting inside a cave of fabric, and his muscled chest pushed against the buttons. It was clear who got *all* the best genes and who got the bargain-bin parts. Everett was *so* glad he decided to go out so he could end up feeling inadequate as fuck.

Exactly what I needed. "Where are we going?" Everett asked.

"The Purple Dream," Roman said as he put his car in reverse.

"The strip club?" Everett's eyes widened. He was completely unprepared for such an adventure. Did Roman really think he'd be able to crawl out of his serial depression for some tits and ass? Everett wasn't *like* Roman.

"That's the one." Roman grinned as he peered over his shoulder.

"I thought we were going to a club!" Everett rubbed his forehead. He hadn't been to a strip club since his bachelor party. His brother had been at the helm then as well. Everett lifted his arms and shook out his shirt, trying to air out his nerves.

"I mean, it's *technically* a club." Roman smirked. "Nice accessory, by the way. How'd you fuck up your hand?"

"I don't want to talk about it," Everett mumbled.

They made the rest of the drive in silence and pulled into the parking lot. A flashing purple sign welcomed them. Everett tried to get into his old mindset. He used to visit these clubs more often than he wanted to admit. He wallowed in the attention of the dancers, trying to tell himself he was special to them. The unfortunate truth for him—and all the other sad saps—was that he was just an ATM with a hard dick. He only stopped going once he met Renee, the sweet bartender at that very club. Her endearing personality drew him to her, and he found himself buying a disgusting drink just to hear her voice.

"If it has to be a strip club, does it need to be the one where I met Renee? I don't see how this will be good for me," Everett said with his hand on the door handle.

"They've redone the entire interior. The only thing they kept the same is the sign out front. And Candy. She really needs to retire." Roman grimaced.

They headed into the club. The flashing lights were disorienting but also somehow invigorating. He could feel the flirty beast rising back to the surface despite the anchoring feeling of grief. A fit blonde woman rocked her hips on stage, her full breasts glistening beneath the lights. Loud, erotic music pumped bass into the room, fueling her gyrations. A topless waitress passed by and placed a fleeting touch on Everett's waist. Familiar aromas filled his nose, somehow sweet as well as sweaty. Like sex and lip gloss.

When Everett turned toward the bar, his breath hitched. Though they'd redone the layout of the club, the back of the bar hadn't changed. The thought of Renee's hands on those taps as she rushed to get another drink to a customer sucked the saliva from his mouth. He definitely needed a drink now.

"Can I get two beers please?" he said toward a gruff, bald bartender. At least he didn't look like Renee.

Everett paid for the beers and scanned the room for Roman. His brother had taken a table right in front of the stage. Of course. He walked to the table and handed a beer to his brother. Everett finished his in several sloppy gulps, dropping the empty glass onto the sticky table. Roman chose to nurse his drink.

"What's your poison tonight?" Roman asked as his eyes searched the room like a predator hunting for prey. The women were clearly not their A-team, but they were friendly, and he desperately needed the distraction.

"Her," Everett said as his eyes fell on a tall brunette. Everett walked over to her, and she gave him a less than friendly glance. No one came to a club like that for the customer service. He cleared his throat. "How much for a dance?" he asked, trying to resurrect his old flirty tact, but he could tell he fell short when her lip just twitched in response.

"It's usually fifty, but for you, I'd do twenty-five," she finally said.

He wasn't naïve to this game. Her price was always twenty-five. He wasn't special, but it allowed him to almost feel like something more than what he was.

"Yes, I want that," Everett said much too quickly. He closed his eyes. *Smooth. Slow down, desperado.* He took a deep breath. "I would like that."

She reached a well-manicured hand toward him, and he shoved his good hand into hers, tucking the burn victim behind his back. She guided him toward a back room. As they passed the stage, men focused on the woman dancing on the pole, whipping out bills without even looking at the denominations. He remembered that reckless focus fondly.

His dancer cleared her throat, forcing his attention back to the task at hand. She spread deep red curtains and led him into the small room. Everett watched the seductive sway of her hips as she walked in front of him. She knew how to move to draw attention to her best assets.

The room was just big enough for two people: a man and a dancer. An armless chair upholstered in purple crushed velvet sat against the wall. A dim light dangled from the ceiling, casting enough of a glow to catch on every curve while disguising any imperfections.

"What's your name?" he asked.

She pushed him into the chair. "Eva," she purred, running a hand over his face as she caressed his cheek. He sighed and leaned into her touch. Desperation wasn't a good look here, but he was too exhausted to play it cool. It felt like forever since he'd been touched.

Eva unclipped her black bra, let it slip down her arms, and draped it on a hook beside her. Her breasts were full, round, and clearly altered.

I hate fake tits, but beggars can't be choosers.

The music skipped for a moment before starting—a soft, melodic tone, perfect for slow dancing. Eva's hips rocked slowly as she leaned over him. Everett kept his hands pinned at his sides; he knew the etiquette.

"You can touch," she whispered as she turned.

Her black underwear rose high on her hips and left little to cover her full ass. He hesitated for a moment, remembering the big neon sign that made sure no man touched the merchandise. She moved her hair over her shoulder and looked back at him with a sly, encouraging smile, and he felt his inhibitions dissolve like ice in boiling water. She turned around and straddled his lap. Her breasts were nearly touching his face—tempting mounds begging for his lips. He leaned away a bit. There was no way he'd put his mouth on them. How many faces had been buried between them tonight alone?

"Wow," a sultry, familiar voice said.

Everett snapped his attention to the left so fast that he pulled a muscle in his neck. Renee stood beside him, her eyes wide. He jumped to his feet and sent Eva spilling onto the floor. She hit the ground with a thud and started to scream.

"Jesus fuck!" Everett shouted as he tried to help her to her feet.

She slapped his hands away and scooted backward as if he'd tried to kill her, running off with panicked whimpers.

"Renee, what the fuck are you doing here?" he whispered in a raspy voice. He covered his crotch with his hands.

"You thought of me." She shrugged.

"I know for a fact I did not think of you with some broad's tits in my face!" he screamed at her.

"You did. You thought about me at the bar. You remembered how we met."

"And you decide to pop up *now*? In the middle of—"

"Okay, that's enough." A large man pushed the curtains aside and grabbed Everett's arm in his meaty fist. "Eva said you pushed her. Time to go!"

I probably look like a psychopath. Everett shook his arm out of the guard's grasp. "I'm going, I'm going," he said. He looked back at Renee and shook his head. All he wanted was *one* night to forget that he was a struggling widower.

Everett walked with the bodyguard toward the main floor. Roman stopped the woman grinding on his lap, and his mouth dropped open. He pushed her aside and stood up, chasing after his brother.

"What happened?" Roman asked.

"Renee happened."

"What?" Roman followed him out the front doors with confusion plastered across his face. "Sir, what happened?" he asked the bodyguard. Even as tall and muscular as Roman was, the bouncer still towered over him.

He shrugged. "He pushed one of the dancers to the ground."

"I did not push her!" Everett yelled as he leaned against the car.

"I'm sorry, my brother is grieving the death of his wife. It was too soon to get him out here again," Roman said as he nodded to the bouncer. He turned back to Everett as he opened the driver's side door and got inside. "What has gotten into you?"

Everett slammed the door. "I told you I didn't want to go here." His shoulders fell forward, and he dropped his face into his hands. Renee had vanished again. How convenient.

They drove back to Everett's house in silence. The only sounds were the revving of the engine and the traffic around them. There was nothing to talk about. He couldn't very well explain that his dead wife cock blocked him.

The moment they pulled into the driveway, Everett got out without speaking and slammed the car door. Roman eased out of the driveway without even shouting goodbye.

Everett entered the house, flopped on the couch, and held back a torrent of frustrated tears. "Renee! Stop fucking with me!" he yelled into the silence. "Just stop," he whispered.

The house was silent, and he was alone.

CHAPTER SIX

E verett woke up in bed. He didn't remember the walk to the bedroom, but somehow he'd made it. He blinked heavily and took a deep breath as he tried to will away the memory of last night. He put his feet flat on the cold hardwood floors before dropping his head into his hands.

"I fucking tried to have a good time, Renee." He took a deep breath. "I tried to move forward with my life, but you just keep showing up." He lifted his head and looked around the empty room. "I need you to stop coming around!" Everett yelled into the stillness. It pained his heart to say it, to even think that way, but he couldn't live like this. Some people would be ecstatic to have their departed spouse remain after death, but she was a constant reminder of how he'd failed his marriage.

Everett stood and pulled on a pair of sweatpants and a t-shirt. There was a hole in the armpit, but it would have to do. He looked out the window. Sunshine peeked at the world from behind a smattering of fluffy clouds. Birds flitted through the trees and bopped around the grass, looking for bugs to devour. It looked so cheery out, which was the oppo-

43

site of how he felt. A gray day with torrential downpour would better match his mood.

He walked toward the front door and put on his sneakers. It'd been a while since he'd gone on a run, and he hoped the fresh air would do him some good. When he opened the door, he took a deep, cleansing breath, inhaling the warm, dry air. He slipped his earbuds into his ears and took off at a slow jog down the street. Sweat developed around his chest and the arch of his back, saturating his shirt. His lungs begged for him to stop, but Renee always told him to push through it because eventually he'd stop feeling the pain.

Would his grief work the same way? If he persevered through the hurt, would it eventually close the hole in his heart?

Doubt it.

Everett felt a familiar presence beside him, but he shook his head and told himself to keep running. When he had to stop at an intersection to look for oncoming traffic, he saw Renee beside him, her hair pulled up in a messy bun. Her mouth moved, but he could hardly hear the buzz of her voice over his music. He turned the volume up, drowning her out completely.

"Nope, not today, Satan," he said out loud, making Renee stop mid-step, her mouth agape.

The loop back to his street was just over two miles long, and he slowed to a walk as he approached his road. He put his hands on his hips and waited for his heart rate to return to a normal pace. For a moment, he worried he'd keel over and end up in limbo beside Renee. Sweat dripped down his face and drenched the rest of his shirt.

He walked into his house, took off his shirt, and wiped his forehead with it. A buzz of adrenaline worked its way through his system. He headed toward the bathroom and turned on the shower. Steam swirled around him. His sweatpants clung to his thighs as he took them off and climbed into the shower. A warm, humid breath rolled from his lips as he leaned back against the wall. The water flowed down his face and chest and carried his sanity toward the drain, and there was nothing he could do about it.

"Everett?"

His eye twitched, and he didn't respond. He dropped his head against the shower wall.

"Why are you ignoring me?" Renee whined.

Everett took a deep breath. "I can't do this." He never thought in a million lifetimes he'd be breaking up with his dead wife.

"Do what?"

"Deal with you being here. You show up whenever I try to be alone. You tell me I need to move on with my life, yet you make that impossible. You're making me paranoid! I never know when you're going to show up. You say it's when I think of you, but I know there are times I haven't."

"I know and I'm sorry, but I'm stuck here!"

"I don't think you are."

Everett turned off the shower but didn't step out. He knew her presence was there without looking outside the curtain. "Can you please leave so I can get out?"

"I've seen you naked, Everett. I'm your wife."

"Please leave!" he snapped. Everett hesitated before sneaking a look past the curtain. Renee was gone, and only an empty feeling remained in the room. He stepped out of the shower and walked toward his bedroom, leaving wet footprints behind him. After slipping into his pajamas, he went to the kitchen and grabbed a beer from the fridge.

The can hissed when he popped the top, and he pressed the cold metal to his lips and guzzled the frigid liquid. He needed something to take the edge off, and beating his dick was off the table. It was hard to pleasure himself when his wife could materialize beside him at any moment. Gone were the days of rubbing one out in peace.

He looked around sheepishly before he pulled his phone from the coffee table and typed "psychics near me" in the search bar. An overwhelming list of mediums populated the results. Embarrassed for himself, he shook his head.

"This is crazy." He put his phone down, waited for a moment, then picked it up again. Everett clicked the name at the top of the list and looked at the website. Crystals with glitter animations lined the sides of the page. A woman with too much mascara and not enough eyeball stared back at him with a thin smile. He argued against himself before finally selecting the Contact Me link on the page. His phone vibrated with an email.

I knew you were going to message me. I will be in touch soon, the message read.

Everett rolled his eyes.

"What am I doing?" he asked himself out loud. It wasn't like him to believe in the hippy-dippy stuff. This was Renee's territory. Everett leaned on the side of science, and none of that psychic stuff was tangible, touchable, or believable.

The doorbell rang, making Everett jump. He closed his tabs like he'd been looking up fetish porn instead of psychic mediums. When he peeked through the blinds, he saw Roman's black sports car in his driveway.

"Hello, Roman," Everett said solemnly as he opened the door. He passed through the foyer, returned to the couch, and chugged the rest of his beer.

Roman followed him and looked around the living room. "Are you okay?"

"No. I think I'm losing my mind." Everett rubbed the back of his neck. He didn't just *think* he was losing his mind, he *knew* he was. The clock ticked on the wall, a loud *click* marking every second. "I keep seeing Renee. Everywhere."

Roman eased his muscular body onto the couch. "That's understandable. Everything will remind you of her for a while, but it'll get easier."

"That's not what I mean," he said with a shake of his head. "I'm *seeing* her, Roman. And hearing her voice."

"That's impossible, Everett." Roman laughed.

Between the two, Everett always had the most vivid imagination, even when they were kids. Imaginary friends were his frequent playmates, but he'd grown out of that. Renee wasn't imaginary.

"I thought so too, but clearly it isn't impossible. She was at the funeral, the strip club, and even on my run with me earlier."

Roman reached out and touched his shoulder. "Maybe you need to talk to someone about this."

"No!" Everett jumped to his feet and paced. "I don't need to go to a counselor, Roman! I just need you to tell me that it's real and that I'm not going crazy."

"I can't do that." Roman tried to stop Everett's pacing by blocking his path with his immovable body. The man probably lived at the gym. "Are you sure you should go to work tomorrow?" he asked with a genuine look of concern.

"I have to."

"Well, at least consider seeing a therapist or visiting a grief group or something."

Everett scoffed. "This isn't grief, Roman. How can I grieve when she's still hanging around?"

Roman cleared his throat and looked away. "I, uh . . . I need to get going. I just stopped in to check on you. Think about getting some help. I'm serious."

His brother had never been one to stick it out through something difficult, and Everett felt like an idiot for sharing his problems with him. What had he expected from him?

Comfort and understanding? That wasn't in Roman's wheelhouse.

"Yeah, I'll think about it," Everett said as he walked him to the door.

Back in his living room, he lifted the phone again and searched for grief counseling. He found a local group that met weekly, and they had a meeting scheduled for that evening at a local church. With a light buzz running through his veins, Everett thought it might not be such a bad idea.

EVERETT LOOKED at himself in the mirror. His hair was a mess, and his clothes weren't much better. An orange SpaghettiOs stain brightened the hem of his white t-shirt, and his dingy gray sweatpants looked like they'd seen better days. That's about all the effort he was willing to put into his appearance. After all, he was going to a group filled with grieving people, and someone was bound to be in worse shape than he was.

He climbed into his Prius and made the short drive to the little church where the group held their weekly meetings. *What am I doing?* he asked himself as he pulled into the parking lot. He looked up at the towering building and then down at the Virgin Mary statue welcoming him inside.

"You should go in." Renee appeared beside him with a smile.

Everett shook his head. "How can a group of grieving people help me get over my grief?"

"It's about feeling heard and knowing other people understand the pain. Go in and try it. I'll come with you."

"Pretty ironic, eh? I wonder if anyone else gets to bring their dead loved one with them."

Everett walked through the glass door and followed a shitty handwritten sign. It wasn't even spelled right.

BEREVE-
MENT
GROUP
←

He looked back at Renee with a pinched expression, and she shrugged. Everett pushed open the heavy metal door, and it slammed behind him, causing a boom to resound through the fellowship hall. The group turned to stare at him. *Sorry,* he mouthed as he went to the back row and took a seat.

A man standing in front of the group shot daggers at Everett with his eyes. "As I was saying, I lost my wife in a boating accident. We were all drinking and she fell off the deck of our yacht."

Renee laughed. Everett snapped his gaze to her, his eyes wide.

"What?" she asked. "She died while riding on their yacht. I'll never be on a yacht, let alone die on one."

"When she hit the water, the boat just rolled right over her," the man continued. "The prop caught her as we passed and . . . and this is all that was left." He lifted a decorative urn with tears in his eyes.

"Looks like you weren't the only one to bring your dead loved one," Renee said with a snicker.

Everyone clapped for the man as he walked back to his seat. An older gentleman passed him, taking his time to adjust his clothes before speaking.

"My name is Sampson, and I lost my wife to terminal cancer."

"Okay, that one's genuinely sad," Renee said.

Sampson regaled the audience with stories of how they

met, leaving the room in tears when he finally detailed her passing. Even Renee cried ethereal tears. Everett was the only dry eye in the room. He couldn't relate to these people and their grief because he didn't share their experience. His wife continued to linger by his side, halting his mourning period and holding him hostage in his own version of purgatory.

A woman in her thirties raised her hand next and made her way to the front of the room as Sampson shuffled back to his seat. She tucked her curly orange hair behind her ears and pulled a tissue from the pocket of her khaki shorts. Dabbing at her red-rimmed eyes, she sucked back a rivulet of snot and began her spiel.

"Hello, I'm Alex. This is my first meeting here. I lost my son, Sam, in a car accident. He was nine years old." Fresh tears welled in her eyes. "I try to remind myself of all the good times we had and how he lived longer than any of my other children."

People in the room shifted in their seats. Child loss was always an uncomfortable topic. He and Renee had talked about having kids, but they kept waiting for his schedule to slow down so he would have time to be there for her. When it never did, they stopped talking about it.

"I lost one to poisoning, and another was mauled by a coyote in my backyard. Just picked up and carried away. He was only a baby." Sobs racked her chest before she continued. "I swore I wouldn't have another child, but then Sam came along." She dabbed at her eyes. "Nine years wasn't long enough."

"How many kids did this woman kill?" Renee asked, her eyes following the woman as she went back to her seat.

The group leader looked at Everett. "You, you're new. Do you care to share?"

Everett pointed to himself and shook his head. *Hard no.*

"Not a fucking chance." Renee laughed. "You'd take my

way out before talking in front of people about your feelings."

"Shut up," Everett whispered.

The man kept pushing Everett. "It's very therapeutic to talk to strangers about how a death has affected you."

"No thanks."

"If you can introduce yourself, you might feel the urge to say more!"

Everett drew a deep breath.

"Oh no," Renee whispered as Everett rose from his chair.

He was here to give this a shot, so he needed to do his part. Maybe the grief he refused to acknowledge played a part in Renee's situation. As he walked to the front of the room, he thought of what to say.

"Hi, I'm Everett . . ."

He couldn't do it. He couldn't discuss how he really felt about what his wife had done, because he hadn't taken the time to process it and understand what he felt. So he gave them what he could. The facts. "My wife killed herself and it sucks. Thanks."

He walked back to his seat as gasps rippled through the crowd.

The group leader stood from his seat and clapped his hands together. "That's all we have time for during our sharing hour today. Let's spend the rest of the session communicating with others and enjoying some of those wonderful oatmeal cookies Eunice blessed us with this week." He pushed his glasses up his crooked nose and motioned toward the back of the room.

Everett rose to his feet and retreated to the table near the back wall. He grabbed a grainy cookie off the table and bit into it. Renee walked beside him, a solemn expression on her face.

The young woman with the dead children walked over to

Everett and pulled a cookie from the tray. "I'm sorry about your wife," she whispered.

"Sorry about your son," Everett said with a full mouth of overcooked oatmeal and molasses.

"Wanna see a picture?"

Instead of declining like he wanted to, he offered a polite nod. The woman pulled out her phone, fighting tears as she scrolled through pictures on the screen. She turned it over to show him. His eyes widened at the picture, and brown crumbs sprayed past his lips from the force of his laughter.

"It's a fucking cat!" He sighed in relief. "She isn't killing human children, it's fine!" he yelled toward the crowd. The woman stared at him, mortified. "I mean, it's a really cute cat, and I'm still sorry for your loss, but I thought you were a sociopath for a minute."

Renee screamed as a cat jumped from the woman's backpack and ran across the floor with its squealing owner running behind it.

The group leader chased after them, waving the cookie in his hand as he spoke. "We don't allow animals in the fellowship hall!"

"He's an emotional support animal! I have rights!" the woman yelled.

Everett stared at the mayhem, his lips tightening. "I'm going to go now. Good luck with . . . everything." He gave the group an awkward wave before hurrying away with Renee in tow.

As Everett opened the door, the cat darted between his legs and froze. *Shit*. He squatted down and tried to make kissy noises toward it. With its ears laid back and its eyes wide, it let out a wild hiss and bolted straight ahead. Had the cat gone left, it would have wound up in a small group of trees. Had the cat gone right, it only had a short jog through the parking lot before it reached what must have been the pastor's house. But the cat chose to go straight, right into a busy street.

Cars slammed on their brakes and swerved to miss the terrified animal, nearly crashing into each other in their efforts. Everett closed his eyes and looked away until the sounds of screeching stopped. The woman released a guttural scream and fell to her knees by the roadside. He looked back at the unfolding disaster and from where he stood, he spotted the cat on the opposite side of the road, alive and well.

"You almost lost another kid, lady!" Everett yelled to the woman. "You should probably go get him! He made it to the other side of the road!"

"Eli, come back!" She ran through traffic the same way her cat had, narrowly becoming road pizza herself.

That was enough excitement for one day. Everett slid into his Prius and made the drive home with his dead wife by his side. "Berevement" groups definitely weren't for him.

CHAPTER SEVEN

Life kept going, even when it seemed like it stopped. Everett raised the knot in his tie and nestled it under his shirt collar. He brushed his hands down the sides of his jacket and hid the wrinkles in his dress shirt beneath the fabric as he buttoned it.

"You got this," Everett told himself as he put putty in his hair, gently brushing it back. He took a deep breath as he tried to prepare himself for the exaggerated condolences, hugs, and eggshell stepping he would face at work. People he hated—and who hated him in return—would be overly kind and sickeningly sweet. Worst of all, they would draw Renee's memory toward the forefront of his mind when he needed her to be in the farthest recesses possible. That spelled disaster. He couldn't look crazy at his job. He got paid to deal *with* the crazies, not be one himself.

Everett grabbed his mug and walked out the door. Anxiety tightened like a belt around his chest with every familiar action: the sound of the car unlocking, the engine humming to life, the car reversing down the driveway and drawing him closer to the law office.

He drifted toward his job in a state of highway hypnosis. A blank canvas filled his mind with each passing mile until he slid his Prius into his reserved parking spot. He remembered nothing of the trip. He took a deep breath before stepping out of the car and grabbing his briefcase from the passenger seat.

The big glass doors hummed as they opened automatically and welcomed him into the air-conditioned building. Everything looked so normal—just how he left it the night of the *incident*, as if he were the only one left ravaged in the midst of a tornado. The security guard at the desk nodded to him without rising to his feet, and his eyes immediately dropped back to his phone. No condolences were shared. No sympathetic glances were exchanged. Everett enjoyed that moment of normalcy.

He took the elevator to the fourth floor. The doors spread open, as did the eyes of every coworker in the room as he emerged from the metal box. The secretary he didn't particularly like stood and offered her condolences as she slid a small stack of files toward him. While he wallowed in misery at home, the criminals kept living it up.

Everett kept his head down as he walked toward his office, but he got caught in several hugs on the way. *I hate hugs, and I hate being touched by grimy hands.* The only hug he needed was from Renee, and she'd stolen that comfort from him.

The door to his office seemed to grow farther away, so he quickened his steps. When he finally reached the entrance to safety, he snatched the door's handle and darted inside before anyone else could reach him. He closed the door and retreated to his desk. Tears loomed behind his eyes, searing his sinuses as he held them back, but he couldn't cry here. The walls were made of glass, and everyone already saw him as weak.

He sat in his leather chair and looked around as if he were in a room he'd never been in before. Everything felt so foreign and disconnected. His eyes landed on the picture of Renee. She smiled up at him, her skin rosy and beautiful instead of pale and lifeless. Yes, this was his office—the place he spent more time than his own home—and that was his dead wife. He turned the photo away from him.

"Are you okay?" Renee asked beside him.

It startled Everett, but not nearly as much as it used to. He was becoming accustomed to her visits.

"I'm not," he said as he wiped a tear that snuck past his eyelid.

Renee looked at him, surely seeing the hollowed-out shell of the man who was once her husband. The soft bags under his eyes made him look older, and his wrinkled suit indicated his lack of domestic intelligence, which was only slightly more refined than that of a toddler.

He fidgeted in his chair. It was hard enough to allow her to see him in such a sorry state, but her presence in his office gave way to new anxieties. He still blamed himself and his long hours for her death, especially since she couldn't articulate her reasons for offing herself. He didn't want her to witness the reminders of what brought them to this place.

Her brown eyes roamed around his work environment, glimpsing an intimate view of his home away from home. "There's so much hustle and bustle here. It's no wonder you were always so anxious," she said as her hand reached out and passed through the overturned picture frame.

"I really can't deal with you here right now, Renee. This is too much. This is all too much," he said as he gestured around the room with his hands.

"How do you think I feel?" Renee asked. "At least you can still do as you please. I'm stuck in an endless white room unless you think of me, and even then, I'm only able to go

57

where you go. I've gotten better about staying away to give you space, but sometimes I need a break."

"Whose fault is that, Renee? Hmm? Who slit her fucking wrists in the bathtub for a reason that isn't even important enough to remember?" He thrust his hand forward and raised his eyebrows.

Renee closed her eyes and dropped her head. "Everett, I—"

His boss knocked on the office door. The big *glass* office door surrounded by glass fucking walls. Everett swallowed his embarrassment. If she—or anyone else—had seen him talking and gesturing to no one, he'd be dismissed for sure.

"Come in!" He motioned to her.

Maria came through the doorway with her full lips shaped into a small, nervous smile. Dark, wavy hair framed her face, stopping just above her shoulders. A snug black pencil skirt hugged her curves, and her large breasts pulled at the buttons of her white top, revealing a peek of the lacy white bra beneath. Out of habit, Everett looked away. He'd always been a faithful husband—aside from his small slip with his ex.

But he wasn't a husband anymore, and Renee had vanished from the room.

"Hey, Everett. Tom said he saw you talking to yourself in here. Are you okay?" She tiptoed around the eggshells as if they were landmines and the office was a fucking battlefield.

Everett shook his head and took a breath. He couldn't explain Renee's presence without sounding like a lunatic. His brother didn't even believe him. Shit, sometimes *he* didn't even believe it himself.

"I'm okay, Maria. This is just an adjustment."

"I'm sure it is. I don't know if you're the type of person who likes to keep distracted with work, but the files are building up." She tried to force an uncomfortable smile as she hinted that he had no choice but to put his nose back to the grindstone.

"I know. I got some already." He held up the stack sitting on his briefcase. "I'll get right to work."

"If you don't think you can do this so soon, Everett . . ."

The world didn't stop because Everett lost his wife. People still needed defense attorneys, and that was Everett's chosen profession, even if he was unfit in his current state.

"I'm fine," he said through a forced smile. A painfully uncomfortable silence filled the space between them as Everett mindlessly shuffled the manilla folders.

"Okay, well, see you at lunch," she finally said. She nodded at him before leaving his office.

Everett grabbed the folders and laid them on the desk. He lifted one and flipped to the first page. Armed burglary. He eyed a picture of his client, caught on store security cameras as he committed the crime. He looked *at* the camera and made no attempt to hide his face. He flipped to the next image. In this one, his client seemed to be adjusting his hair with his left hand as he gazed into the large round mirror right beside the camera. His right hand gripped a small black pistol. A tattoo ran across his knuckles. It probably spelled out something really dumb—and damning, considering it tied him to the crime without doubt.

He closed the folder and opened the second one in the stack. Hit and run with the victim's hair and blood stuck in the grill of his client's car. Cameras aimed at the street caught his drunk ass swerving for three blocks with visible blood on the white hood of the car. And was that a bottle of liquor tipped into his mouth in that last photo? Everett groaned and closed the file.

The third folder told the story of domestic assault. A jealous ex-girlfriend stormed into the apartment and repeatedly stabbed the victim in the arms . . . in front of a pastor who was there to counsel him after his mother had passed. With such a credible witness, this case looked just as grim as the rest. Still, he flipped to the next page. The client's rap sheet of previous assaults unfolded before him like an unending scroll.

Everett sighed. "Losing cases. All of them." He brushed a frustrated hand through his hair. He was at the point in his career where he was struggling to defend such clearly guilty clients. His poker face wasn't as unflappable as it used to be, and sympathy was becoming a struggle for him with each passing day. If he couldn't pretend to believe them, the juries sure wouldn't, and getting lesser sentences seemed about as possible as shitting a gold brick.

His best friend at work knocked on the door and pulled him away from his pity party. Everett sighed as he motioned him in. It wasn't that Everett didn't want to see Clarke, but he really did not fucking want to see Clarke. He wasn't in the right headspace to deal with his high energy, which was a lot for most people on the best days. The guy was over thirty yet locked in a perpetual frat-boy mentality.

"Everett! I'm glad you're back. How're you holding up?"

"I'm fine, Clarke. Clearly," Everett said as he motioned to the files in front of him.

Clarke walked closer and leaned over his desk, flipping through the files. Even in this position, the swoosh in his blond hair remained in place. His dark blue eyes scanned the folder, and he pursed his lips in a low whistle. "You've got your work cut out for you with these."

"You're telling me," Everett mumbled.

"Hey, remember that guy who was doing the home robbery and ended up in the emergency room after the home-owner's dog mauled him? They had his fingerprints, his blood on the scene, and his hospital admission, but I *still* got him off on a technicality! A fucking technicality!" Clarke almost exploded with self-indulgent excitement.

Lucky you. I couldn't find a technicality if it bit me in the dick. "Wow, I didn't think you'd get that thrown. The judge is . . . something. And I'm not even sure Prosecutor McNinch is a human being." Everett feigned excitement for his friend. That's what friends did. Normal ones, at least.

"I know! I was as surprised as my client."

"How have you done this so long, Clarke?" Everett asked as he rubbed his forehead. "How do you help all these blatant criminals get off, day after day?"

"Well, Everett, everyone has a right to due process. And it pays my bills. Besides, bigwigs are just starting to take notice of me. If I have to let some schmucks out to advance myself, I won't lose sleep over it." Clarke shrugged. "Getting soft on us?"

"No, but I haven't won a case in a while. I'm questioning all my life choices with everything that happened. It's hard to think any of this was worth what I lost."

"You're having a dry spell. It'll rain soon. Maybe not with these cases—yikes—but I know it's coming." He smiled at Everett, giving the good ol' college try at cheering him up.

It wasn't working.

"Maybe we should grab lunch today," Clarke continued. "I know you probably aren't ready to start dating again, but I know a really cute waitress at Tucker's Pub that's good for a flirt session." He gave him a wink.

That was Clarke. Always thinking with his dick. Then again, Renee said moving on might be the way to send her to the great beyond . . .

Everett shook his head. "Maybe some other time. I'm not quite ready yet."

Clarke raised his hands. "No prob, no prob. Just let me know when you're ready and we'll chase some tail."

"We'll get together for drinks soon, but I really need to focus on work." Everett faked a smile. The mental exhaustion made it difficult to offer much more than that.

Clarke finally took the hint and left his office. Everett tried to look busy to avoid any more company, from the living or the dead.

CHAPTER EIGHT

E verett woke up and rubbed his hand down his face with an exhausted sigh. He was surrounded by loose files and paperwork strewn across his bed. He groaned as he wiped his eyes.

He'd fallen asleep while trying to find holes in his cases. Any hole, no matter how small. Anything that would put a hint of doubt in a juror's mind. He picked up a piece of crumpled paper labeled Coroner's Report and tried to stretch it flat again. He'd tossed and turned on it as he slept.

"Real professional," he whispered to himself. He shouldn't have brought his work home like this but being in the office wasn't working. Pretending he was a normal human being wasn't working.

Everett looked down at the unmade bed and frowned. Renee would always make their bed every morning. In the time it took him to drag himself to the bathroom and prepare for a day of work, she'd tuck and turn down the bedding until it looked just so. He gave her shit about it because he couldn't understand the point of making a bed if you were just going to sleep in it again and mess it all up. Now he realized how much that little gesture meant. Like there was some semblance of normalcy or order in the home. As if crawling into a made bed helped you feel like you had your shit more together than you actually did.

The passing thought was enough to draw Renee beside him. It was the first time he'd viewed her arrival. She didn't materialize in a flash like he'd imagined, but a shimmering moment as her body formed, as if she was being pulled from the other realm and downloaded into this one. Television made it seem so much more instantaneous.

"Evening," she said.

She stared at Everett, his messy hair reaching out in every direction toward the sky. His five o'clock shadow was prominent, something he never would have allowed in their life together. No matter how busy he was or how little time he had, he prioritized his morning shave. He rubbed his hands through his hair, flattening it. He couldn't do a damn thing about the stubble on his face. The razor didn't hold importance anymore. Nothing did. Besides, most widowers probably looked like this. Unless they offed their spouse themselves or held no fondness in their heart for the recently departed. And he actually *liked* Renee.

"Are you okay?" she whispered. Her eyes darted to the iron, and it made Everett feel like a bigger pile of steaming shit.

He tugged down the wrinkled dress shirt. "No, I'm not, Renee. My job is terrible and my life is a mess without you here."

"It's not a mess." She tried to comfort him, but her plastic smile was translucent. "Okay, it's a little messy. That suit is . . . it really needs a dry cleaner or something. You can't go to court like that."

"Can you help me iron it?" He sat up and looked at her with a hint of desperation in his voice. He tried to YouTube how to do it, but watching the video and handling the iron at the same time had only resulted in another burn.

"No, I can't pick up or move anything."

"Can't ghosts move objects, lift things . . . push an iron?" He rubbed his forehead.

"I'm not a typical ghost, Everett. I can't lurk around and have my own free will. I'm tethered to you and even then, it's only when you think of me. I don't have ghoulish desires to scare people." She chuckled. "Any luck with those cases?" She looked at the explosion of paperwork on their bed.

"In the hit and run, the *only* thing they didn't do by the books was the breathalyzer. But whether his BAC was zero or point-five, the evidence still shows he hit the person. The fucking piece of scalp on the grill of his car makes this case open and shut."

"Could you argue he may not have been the one behind the wheel?"

Everett pursed his lips as he dug through the case files. He pulled a picture out and laid it on the crumpled pillow so Renee could see it.

"Time stamped, ten minutes before the accident occurred." Everett stared at the picture taken by the traffic camera of his wide-eyed and crazy client as he ran the light going eighty-five in a forty.

"Ouch," Renee whispered.

"Ouch is right. Pardon me while I go off myself." He shuffled the files together to take them off the bed before realizing what he'd said. "Oh, Renee, I'm sorry."

"Don't apologize. It's fine. I don't even remember it." Her smile was pinched.

Must be nice. Everett remembered all of it. The warm water as he pulled her from the bathtub. The swirl of blood as her cuts leaked out the last of her life. Worst of all, he remembered her very last breath while he panicked on the phone.

He didn't even get to say goodbye to her. Not really . . . unless telling her spirit to leave him alone counted.

"Everett?" She broke his wallowing thoughts with her soft voice.

"What?" He started to unbutton his dress shirt.

"I think you need to go on a date or something. You can't just mope around here all the time . . . looking like this." She gestured to his face.

"I can't go on a date, Renee. Not yet. I'm not ready," he whispered. His shoulders fell forward. He knew he looked like a pathetic person, but he *felt* like a pathetic person, so it fit.

"Please? For me?" she asked with her eyes wide and pleading.

She'd given him that same look when she shot him a teasing glare at the bar all those years ago. But her eyes were lively and vivid then. Now they were dull and almost see-through. Dead.

"I really think I'll be able to move on if you do," Renee said. "I don't know if you have to fall in love or if you just need to get laid, so we'll have to try everything."

"And you're just okay with that?" he asked.

"If it means I can move on, hell yes. I'm tired of lingering."

Everett scratched his chin. If he just needed to get laid, he could always give his ex a call. "What about Christine? She'd be—"

"No."

Everett tossed his hands in the air. "I don't know what I'm supposed to do, then! It's not like I have a little black book of women who are dying to jump into bed with me. Aside from kissing Christine, I was a faithful husband. Loyalty meant a lot to me, and that one indiscretion ate me up inside."

Renee looked at the floor. "Not her."

"Fine," he said with a roll of his eyes. "Got any bright ideas?"

"What about a dating website?"

Everett nodded. "Okay, that doesn't sound too bad. Takes some of the pressure off since I don't have to embarrass myself in public. I can just do it from the privacy of my home."

He walked to the living room and opened his laptop. Used coffee mugs stood like sentries around the table, guarding the machine from the invading horde of food wrappers and crumpled paper towels.

"God, Everett. This is a pigsty."

He ignored her and pulled out a chair so she could sit beside him. He did a Google search for dating sites and clicked on the first one to pop up. Bright colors and images of smiling men and women painted his screen. All of them were insanely attractive, of course. He clicked the button to create an account and started filling in his information.

"Lawyer4You?" Renee said with a laugh. "Can't you come up with something better? This isn't a Yahoo! chat room from 1999."

Everett groaned and deleted the nickname. In the empty space, he typed EndersLaw.

"Now it looks like an advertisement," Renee whispered.

He tapped the delete key with gusto. "What do you suggest, since you seem to be an expert?"

Renee tapped her finger against her lips. "What about EvEnders15?"

"Why fifteen?"

Her jaw dropped. "We were married on the fifteenth!"

"How will I explain that if someone asks? Oh, my ghost wife thought it would be cute?" He typed in EvEnders69 and clicked to the next field. He could almost hear her eyes rolling beside him.

After filling in a page of details about his hobbies, interests, and habits, he reached a page asking what he wanted in a woman. He shifted in his seat. How could he be honest about his likes and dislikes with his dead wife sitting beside him? He liked big, natural breasts. He liked blondes. He liked a woman who didn't mind eating fast food a few times a week. While he loved Renee, she wasn't any of these things, and he didn't want to hurt her feelings by filling in the fields with everything she hadn't been.

He closed the laptop. "Maybe we should finish this up another day. I'm kind of over it for now."

"You're over it? Try sitting in a big white room with nothing to do for eternity unless your husband thinks of you. And even when I'm called to your side, I never know if you'll be happy or annoyed to see me. Isn't there some way we can get you a date tonight?"

He had one option, though he didn't want to use it. With a sigh, he pulled his phone from his pocket and dialed Clarke.

EVERETT TUCKED his blue polo shirt into his khaki pants and stared at his childless "dad bod," complete with a stomach pooch that pushed further past his waistband with every year he aged. He sighed and untucked the shirt, concealing it. His watch ticked on his wrist, and he checked it once more.

"Shit, I'm going to be late. Great first impression," he said as he patted his pocket to check for his wallet.

Everett drove to the restaurant with anxious fingers tapping the steering wheel. This was his first date since he and Renee went out a few months ago, but could that even be considered a date since they were married? He wasn't entirely convinced he knew how to navigate these waters anymore.

We'll find out today.

He drove until the bright sign for Giorgio's Italia came into view. Cars packed the parking lot, and it took several circles around the asphalt to find a spot. Every time he thought he saw an empty slot, it was occupied by a compact car or motorcycle. Sweat brewed on his forehead. He found a less than ideal spot beside a lifted truck with confederate flag mud flaps. Lucky for him—and even though everyone made fun of him for it—his little Prius fit into the tight space.

He checked his face in the mirror once more, wiping sweat off his forehead before hurrying across the large lot at a jog. A driver slammed on their brakes as he accidentally ran across their path.

Shit, I almost wound up beside Renee.

Cool air blasted him as he opened the glass doors. Tinkling piano music floated from somewhere inside the softly lit dining room. Aromas of garlic and thyme infiltrated his nose and traveled straight to his stomach, eliciting a deep grumble from the empty organ. When was the last time he'd eaten a meal?

He walked up to the hostess. "Reservation under last name Enders," he said. He struggled to keep from panting after his jog and near-death experience, and he pretended to look around the dining area as he focused on slowing his breathing.

The hostess checked her tablet. "Yes, looks like the other member of your party arrived twenty-five minutes ago."

Shit, Everett thought as he followed the hostess to a small table in the corner of the room. The colorful glass lamp shade above their table sent a spray of light onto his face, giving his

69

sweaty forehead all the glory. Too nervous to speak, he sat across from his blind date and swiped a napkin across his face, leaving an oily residue on the dark green fabric.

"I'm Tara. You must be Everett?" She brushed a strand of short blonde hair behind her ear.

He'd forgotten to introduce himself in his hurry to sit. He tried to stand again but bumped his head on the lamp in the process. He plopped back down with a sheepish smile. "Yes, I'm so sorry. I haven't been on a date in a long time except with my wife." He cleared his throat and lifted the laminated menu. He couldn't even read the words, but he needed a distraction.

"Your wife?" Her mouth dropped open.

Everett dropped his menu onto the table, nearly knocking over a stagnant glass of water that should have been consumed twenty-five minutes ago. "Oh, no, I'm not married anymore!" He released a nervous laugh. "She's dead."

Tara's face went from annoyed to uncomfortable. "I'm sorry for your loss."

Everett groaned internally. *This girl would probably have a better date with Ed Kemper.*

Renee appeared at the table beside him. He jumped, the tension coursing through his muscles. She was the last person he wanted to witness this trainwreck.

"Did you really just talk about your dead wife five minutes into this date?" Renee groaned. "Politics, religion, dead wives . . . all things you don't talk about on a first date, Everett."

He cleared his throat again and grabbed the glass of water. He gulped down a lukewarm mouthful and sent some dribbling down the side of his mouth and onto his shirt.

"Real attractive," Renee said. "Are you trying to keep me here forever?"

"So, how do you know Clarke?" Everett asked, trying to end the awkward silence between them.

"He was my brother's lawyer."

"Oh, yeah, Clarke's an excellent lawyer. Did he win?"

"No, but we've just kinda been friends ever since."

Everett knew what it meant for her to be Clarke's friend. The women he surrounded himself with all knew how he tasted.

"Oh, yeah." Everett nodded as he eyed the menu again. "Nice restaurant, huh?"

"Yeah, I've never been here before." Her eyes darted around, probably looking for the nearest exit.

"What do you do for work, Tina?"

"Tara! Tara!" Renee shouted beside him.

"Tara, I meant to say Tara." He grabbed the napkin and blotted his forehead again.

She gave him a small smile and nodded as she pulled her phone from her pocket and laid it on the table. "I groom dogs."

"Oh, cool." Everett cleared his throat once more and took another sip of water.

"This is so uncomfortable," Renee said quietly.

A server approached their table. "Are you two ready to order?" he asked.

"Oh, I haven't even looked over the menu yet," Tara said with a pinched smile. "Could you give us ten more minutes?"

The server nodded and walked away.

"She was here by herself for twenty-five minutes and didn't bother to glance at the menu?" Renee said. "I call bullshit."

Everett rolled his eyes.

"I'm sorry. I didn't mean to annoy you," Tara said. She lifted her phone.

"No, no! That eye roll wasn't directed at you," he blurted. "It was . . . the piano music. I hate this song."

Her blue eyes danced back and forth as she typed, ignoring his response. Renee walked behind her chair and peered over her shoulder. Everett wanted to tell Renee to stop invading the poor girl's privacy, but his dead wife's expression made it look like she'd seen a ghost.

Renee sighed and walked over to Everett. She leaned down, her lips so close to his ear that it gave him shivers.

"In five minutes, she'll get a call from her friend. Her dog's sick and she has to go." She drew her lips together.

They sat awkwardly across from each other before Tara's phone rang like clockwork. She answered it with preconceived panic.

"What? Buster? Is he okay?" Her dramatic display sent bile crawling up Everett's throat. "Oh god, I can leave right now and pick him up. I'll be right there."

She scrambled to her feet and snatched up her purse and jacket before she even got off the phone. The server approached the table, but she waved him away.

"Oh, you're leaving?" Everett asked, although he already knew the answer.

"Yeah, my dog is sick and I have to pick him up and bring him to the vet. So sorry to have to cut this short. It's such a shame," she said with a fake smile on her face. She waved awkwardly as she turned and walked out of the restaurant.

Renee sat in the now vacant seat. "That was a textbook escape call," she said with a shake of her head.

"What'd I do wrong?" He sighed. *It might be easier to list what I did right.*

"For starters, you were late. You made her introduce herself first, you mentioned me, you spilled your drink like a toddler, and your conversation skills were at that age level too."

His shoulders dropped. "Wow, okay. I guess I'm not that good at this."

"You never were." Renee laughed as the server approached the table again.

He looked at Everett with a curious lift of his eyebrow. "Who are you talking to?" He removed the menu in front of Renee.

"Me? No one. Can I get the chicken parm, please?" Everett said as he handed his menu over. He'd half expected the date to end as dinner for one.

CHAPTER NINE

E verett sat at his kitchen table and stared at his case files as he opened the cardboard takeout container and shoved a fork into his rice. The pages stared back, mocking him. He blew on a piece of chicken before sliding it past his lips, the sweet sauce tantalizing his taste buds. It was the third time that evening he'd started from the top, scouring the evidence for a flaw. Anything, even the smallest little breadcrumb that could help guide him toward a reduced sentence or dismissal. Everything had been done by the book. *By the goddamn book.* These kinds of cases made prosecutors come in their pants. They could do this trial in their sleep. For defense attorneys, this was more like a nightmare featuring the flapping jaws of a manilla folder stuffed with the files of an unwinnable case.

His phone rang, and he put it on speakerphone without looking at it.

"Hello?" he said with a mouthful of food. He chewed and swallowed.

"I heard the date went awful," Clarke said—much too

fucking loudly. "Can you hear me? I'm on my Bluetooth in the car."

"I can hear you fine," Everett said as he took another bite. *Pretty sure they could hear you in space.*

"So?"

"Yeah, it was terrible. No chemistry." It didn't take a scientist to know that he was like francium—useless, toxic, and unstable as fuck.

"She thinks you're still married."

"I said I wasn't," Everett said.

"I told her you weren't lying about your deceased wife."

Everett tightened his lips. "Thanks, but why did you set me up with someone you hooked up with?"

"I've hooked up with every girl I know." Clarke laughed, and Everett was certain that was probably true. Clarke was a whore.

"I already get your sloppy seconds at work. I don't need to stick my dick in them too."

"Ahh, cruel. I'll see you tomorrow?" he asked.

Where else would I be?

A button clicked as if Clarke had tried to end the call. "Such a sad man," he said before the call dropped.

Everett stopped chewing and stared at the phone. *Rude, but not untrue.*

Unable to take another second of staring at the files, he dropped his fork, gathered his remaining Chinese food, and walked to the living room. He turned the TV to the news and positioned his food on the coffee table. His feet were tucked into moccasin slippers with a tear at the seam, exposing his wool sock. Renee had gotten him a new pair, but they gathered dust as he picked up the moccasins night after night. He was a creature of habit.

The clock under the TV read 9:00 p.m. by the time he shoveled a final forkful of food into his mouth and folded the top of the carton down so he could place it in the fridge for tomorrow.

As he crawled into bed, the expensive bamboo sheets enveloped him and clung to his skin like a hug. He remembered telling Renee there was absolutely no way he would pay the three-hundred-dollar price tag for the sheet set, only to find the bed made with them that evening.

"They are so worth it," Renee said as she appeared beside him.

He didn't jump this time. He was almost beginning to grow fond of her company.

"I would and have slept on ten-dollar sheet sets just fine," Everett said as he rolled over to face her. The silky-soft fabric caressed him.

They sat in silence together. Everett's breaths were slow and even, but there were no sounds coming from Renee. Her chest didn't rise and fall, reminding him she was not from this world any longer.

"Clarke called me a sad man," Everett whispered. The claws of depression reached up and dug into his heart. He was clinical at this point, but he still didn't want to ask for help. He would figure it out like he did everything else . . . kinda.

"You aren't a sad man, Everett."

"I wear slippers while I watch the news, I go to bed at nine o'clock, and I traded my favorite car for a hybrid."

"They're economical with good gas mileage," Renee said with a smile.

"When I told you about wanting an energy-efficient car, you told me you'd die before you'd let me buy one."

"I did say that, didn't I? Guess it kind of rang true. But you aren't a sad man." She reached out her hand to touch Everett, but it went through him. "We need to get you back on the horse. And by horse, I mean a lady friend." She smirked.

"I don't want that."

"I know that's a lie. You miss the touch of a woman."

He stared at her form in awe. She was so human, so present and beautiful. The soft waves in her dark hair and the curves of her hips were exactly what he remembered. "I miss the touch of *you*."

He hadn't appreciated her enough when she'd been alive. Hadn't held her close and cherished her. His time had been wasted on criminals, court appearances, and dead-end cases. And where had it gotten him? No closer to his fucking goal, and now his wife was a ghost.

His phone chimed on the nightstand. With a sigh, he reached over and read the email that had come through. "Fuck," he whispered.

"What's wrong?"

"Prosecution wants to move one of the goddamn cases up. That means I have even less time to find loopholes."

Renee paced the room, her ghostly form passing through objects in her path. "Can't you think about me for once? Can't you stop working long enough to get me out of fucking white-room hell, Everett?"

"Why is this my fault?" He sat up in bed and threw off the covers. He was too steamed to sleep now. "I'm not the one who gargled a fistful of pills and opened my veins. And now you can't even remember *why* you did it. Did you ever think that maybe *you* are the reason you're stuck, Renee?"

"That's not fair," she said. "You haven't even tried to move on, so how can we know that's not the rope tying me to you?"

Everett got to his feet and went to Renee's side of the bed. With his teeth clenched together, he yanked open the drawer of her bedside table and rifled through the contents.

"What are you doing?" she asked.

"Looking for answers." He pulled a notebook from the back of the drawer and flipped through the pages. Empty. "Why the fuck did you keep an empty notebook in here?"

Renee shrugged. "In case I ever thought of something I needed to write down." She walked toward him. "You won't find anything in there. I didn't leave a note."

Rage and frustration simmered to the top and boiled over inside his brain. "How can you remember that you didn't write a note, yet you can't seem to recall why you did this to us?"

When he turned around, she was gone.

He hung his head and stuffed the notebook into the drawer, closing it with a frustrated groan. Maybe Renee was right. Maybe he needed to try harder. Grabbing his phone from the nightstand, he scrolled past the email about work and clicked on the email from the dating site encouraging him to finish his profile. Without Renee looming over his shoulder, he could complete the questionnaire honestly.

After filling in the answers—while looking over his shoulder—he needed to execute the final step. He had to add a picture. He scrolled through his phone, but Renee stood beside him in every image. Flipping backward in time, he watched her smile grow from forced to genuine. In earlier pictures, she looked so happy. And so had he.

Unable to look at the reminders of his failed marriage for a second longer, he clicked the icon for the camera and lifted the phone above his head. He took two pictures. In the first, he smiled, but he kept his face schooled and serious in the second. He looked over the images and grimaced. It wasn't a flattering angle. A blob of skin pooled under his chin in both shots, and his eyes had bags big enough to stuff bodies into. He sat up and tried again, but the lighting made him look ten years older.

How do women do this? I feel like such an ass.

He trudged into the bathroom. Nothing said single and ready to mingle like a mirror shot. He aimed the phone at the mirror and smiled, but his smile morphed into a look of disgust when he glimpsed his stomach. Too many late nights with sugary coffee and donuts had been unkind to his physique. He slipped into a white t-shirt to hide his shame and tried again.

It wouldn't win him any modeling contracts, but it would do. He uploaded the image and activated his account.

CHAPTER TEN

E verett clutched the steering wheel and gritted his teeth as his mind screamed thoughts to Renee, willing her into the backseat. His mother sat in the passenger seat. A bright orange scarf wound around her neck, and her pale gray hair bobbled beside her cheeks whenever she spoke. Her mouth only opened to complain, judge someone else, or a mixture of both.

He glanced in the rearview mirror just as Renee materialized, and a smirk crept onto his face. *If I have to suffer, so do you.* He still wasn't happy with her after their disagreement, and a car ride with her favorite person was just the ticket to really showcase his displeasure.

"Why the hell did you have to think of me right now?" she said with a groan.

"Wipe that ghastly smirk from your face, Everett. You look positively predatory when you do that," his mother said. Without missing a beat, she jumped into her next topic. "You remember Deb from church? When I told her about Renee, she said her son remembered her from that filthy club where she worked. Isn't that funny, dear?"

"Hilarious," Everett said in an even tone. He didn't entirely understand what she thought was funny. Her ramblings tended to draw out and not require active listening. An oncoming big rig could drift into their lane and she wouldn't halt her conversation. If the military had the steadfast staying power of his mother's voice, all wars would be impossible to lose.

"That place was dirty," she said with a grimace.

"Mom, how can you say the place is dirty unless you've been there? And if pious Deb's son saw Renee there, then he was at that *dirty club* too." His knuckles turned white as he continued toward the grocery store.

"I really can't believe she was a bartender," his mother said as she stared out the window.

"What's wrong with bartenders?"

"Yeah, what's wrong with bartenders?" Renee said, mirroring Everett's question. Her eyes squinted at his mother.

Everett's eyes widened, but then he remembered that no one else could hear Renee but him. She could talk as much shit as she wanted.

"They're just so . . . slutty." His mother shook her gray head.

"Slutty?" Renee shrieked. "I've never slept with anyone from my job besides Everett!" She raised her hands toward his mother's neck and made a choking motion with her teeth bared.

"Don't call my wife slutty, Mom," Everett said with a rise in his usual calm demeanor.

"She isn't your wife anymore."

"You're happy she's gone, aren't you? You never wanted me to marry her. Hell, you called her my 'wife person' until a year ago."

"Yeah, I remember that, you haughty bitch," Renee said with a sneer aimed at the back of her head.

"I liked Renee just fine, Everett. I just didn't like her for *you*." She twirled a manicured hand in the air.

"Why wasn't she good enough by your estimation?" Everett's jaw clenched so hard he thought he might break his teeth. His eyes were locked on the road ahead of him, fighting all urges to drive off a bridge and end everyone's suffering.

"She just had no motivation to be anything more than what she was. She didn't push herself. And she didn't push you." His mother tapped her short fingers on the armrest, and somehow even *that* sounded judgmental.

"What's wrong with what I was?" Renee said from the backseat.

Everett made a swift and very illegal U-turn and headed back toward his mother's house. He'd had enough. "It's nice to know what you really thought of my wife."

"What are you doing?" his mother asked.

"Taking you home. I really can't take this kind of negativity from you right now. I'm not your little boy anymore. You would have hated any woman I married because she took me away from you." He paused and sniffed back the tears dancing behind his eyes. "Even someone as perfect as Renee."

He glanced at his wife in the mirror. Her eyes dropped, and her hands wrestled with each other on her lap. Everett drove in silence except for the repetitive huffing coming from his mother's throat.

After he dropped her off, he drove back to his house, stripped off his clothes as soon as he got in the door, and climbed into his bed. He didn't have the energy to do anything else. Renee followed and sat beside him.

"I'm sorry you had to hear all that," he said.

Renee shrugged. "It's not anything I didn't already know. She's always detested me."

"Still . . . I'm sorry."

A realization dawned on him. He had to try harder to help Renee move on. He had to let her go. With this new determination, he closed his eyes and recalled the first time they met. If he planned to find that sort of spark with another woman, he needed to remember what that felt like.

All those years ago, he'd walked out of the back room of the club, adjusting his tie. He and Roman liked to dress up when visiting those establishments because they thought it gave them a leg up on the patrons with mustard stains on their shirts and neckbeards gracing their chins.

He strutted toward the bar and leaned his elbows on the sticky surface. A curvy brunette stood behind the bar, filling drinks and smiling at everyone she locked eyes with. The moment he met her gaze, he was smitten. His eyes roved over her as he fiddled with the buttons on his shirt, concealing his chest hair that had become exposed during a private dance with too much heavy touching. He wanted to look modest and presentable. Or as much as he could after having boobs in his face for the last ten minutes.

"Hey!" Her greeting was as bubbly as the champagne she placed on a tray for a waiting waitress. "What can I get you?" She leaned closer as she yelled over the music, pushing her breasts higher in her Purple Dream tank top. The swells of her chest gleamed with sweat and glitter.

"Uh, make me your favorite drink?" he asked with a smile. He cursed himself for not giving her a gravelly, suggestive request for sex . . . on the beach.

"You sure you want that?" She grinned back at him, brushing her dark hair behind her ear.

"I'm very sure I want that."

"Are we still talking about drinks?" She looked up at him with pouty lips as she poured vodka into a glass.

The way she moved behind the bar made his dick stiffen against his khakis. She leaned over and grabbed the gin and tequila, pouring them both at the same time. She double fisted a bottle of triple sec and rum, and poured enough to nearly fill the glass. In one fluid motion, she leaned down and grabbed the sour mix, topped it off with a splash of Coke, and dropped a few ice cubes in. Her smile was wide, and her eyebrows lifted as she put the drink down on the table, liquid sloshing over the sides. She perched the lemon slice on the rim and passed it to Everett.

"Long Island?" Everett asked.

"I call it a . . . Longer Island. Pure alcohol with just a splash of soda."

He took a sip of the drink, and his face twisted from its strength. He must have looked like a teenager trying his first sip of stolen liquor. Real mature. He coughed, trying to hide it beneath a clearing of his throat. "It's awful," he said with his face still rearranged as he placed it back on the table.

"Fair," she said with a laugh. "Do you want something else?"

"No, I hate it, but I'm going to drink it. How much do I owe you?" he asked as he pulled out his wallet.

"On the house." She gestured to him to put his wallet away. That wasn't the only thing that had been on the house that night, but this meant so much more. She bit her lip as she stared at him. Heat crept across his cheeks.

Renee leaned over the counter and grabbed a napkin, her breasts pressing against the wet surface. He turned his head and looked through the club for his brother. As much as he wanted to stare at her chest, he didn't want to seem like a total perv.

Little late for that, he thought as his eyes landed on a

topless redhead grinding her barely covered lower half against the pole jutting from center stage.

"Hey," the bartender called from behind him.

He turned around and met her eyes again, his heart hammering twice as hard this time.

She held the napkin toward him. "You look like you might need this." A gentle smile pulled at her perfect lips.

Sweat prickled his brow. Had he spilled some of the drink on himself when he'd had his sputtering fit after sipping that gasoline mixture she'd concocted? He took it and wiped at his mouth.

A musical laugh drifted from her. "No, look at the napkin."

He pulled it away from his face and stared in disbelief. She'd written her number and her name across the cheap material. Flushed heat crept down his chest, only half covered by his dress shirt.

"Thank you, Renee." He hesitated for a moment before turning away and going back to meet up with his brother.

He'd texted her that night, unable to observe the suggested twenty-four-hour waiting period. It hadn't mattered to him if he seemed desperate. Because he *was* desperate. To see her again. To hear her laugh again. To get to know her. He'd eventually done all of those things—and more.

When had he fucked up his love story? And how would he ever begin his next chapter?

CHAPTER ELEVEN

"I've got the case of the century for you." Clarke came into Everett's office like a whirlwind and tossed a file onto the table. Everett put down his pen and looked up at him with a hint of suspicion before lifting the folder. He opened it and spread the papers across his desk. His eyes slid down the page and landed at the charge: murder.

Everett's eyes widened as he took in the crime-scene photos just behind the initial page. A very dead woman lay on a bed, surrounded by a halo of blood. Red splatters painted the walls and ceiling, like droplets of paint from a maniacal artist's paintbrush. Gashes and gouges decorated her nude flesh. Her pale lips parted in a death scream, and glassy, unseeing eyes glared through a bluish haze. He pushed the papers away from him.

"If by that you mean the unwinnable case of the century, you'd be right," Everett quipped with a sigh. He loathed murder cases. He didn't get into this job to help murderers escape justice. Every normal cell in his body felt guilty about that, and maybe that was part of the reason he'd remained unsuccessful. He dropped his head into his hands. "He's clearly guilty."

"And it's up to you to make him seem otherwise," Clarke said as he placed his palms on the desk.

"I can't do shit with this case, Clarke. Why can't you guys give this dog a bone just once? Don't tell me the cases aren't there, because they seem to slide across your desk all the time."

"That's not true. Besides, the case assignments don't go through me, bucko. They come from way beyond our pay grade." He pointed toward the boss's office down the hall. Everett cringed. He *hated* when Clarke called him bucko. Almost as much as he hated murder cases.

There was a knock on the door, and Everett looked up to see Maria standing on the other side of the glass. Clarke slapped the file before excusing himself and leaving, motioning Maria inside on his way out.

She closed the door with a soft click and faced him. "Everett, are you okay? You seem upset again."

Everett sighed. "Maria, with all due respect, why did I get this case?" It seemed like a fair fucking question. He felt like he had "sucker" written on his forehead lately.

Maria sat in a chair across from him and tucked her rich brown hair behind her ears. She glanced at the file and winced. "Which one is it?"

"The Ortiz murder."

"Ah, that one." She drew a quick breath. "You don't get anything more than I think you can handle."

"If you think I can handle them, then why do I keep losing every one of these cases?" Everett stood and paced in a tight line. He turned and peered out the massive window over-looking the city below him.

Her voice was low behind him. "You just haven't found your golden case, Everett, but you've come so close. No one notices details like you do. If there's something to find, you'll find it." Maria stood up and walked over to Everett. Her high heels sounded rhythmically on the tiled floor of his office. She touched his arm and squeezed.

He felt guilty for enjoying her touch. While he was supposed to be moving on to help Renee, he still struggled with feeling as if he were cheating on her whenever a woman made his heart—or dick—flutter.

"What was your golden case, Maria?" Everett asked without looking at her.

She hesitated. "I was in court for a murder case five years ago. As I looked through the case file again for shits and giggles, there it was, clear as day. A mental evaluation report for my client. I don't know how I missed it all the times I looked at the file. Once we did a little more digging, he was deemed unfit for trial. Got off on an insanity deal, but he's probably still rotting away in an institution somewhere. He definitely did it, but he's where he needs to be."

Everett turned toward her, his mouth agape. He'd cut his dick off for a break like that. "Wow, lucky," he said with a sigh as he watched the traffic beneath his window. The honks of impatient drivers found their way into his office, even on the fourth floor.

"Wasn't just luck, Everett. So many cases will have somewhere where someone fucked up," she said, trying to reassure him. "A good defense attorney will find that mistake and exploit the shit out of it. Ideally, before they're in the middle of a trial like I was."

"I don't know that I *want* to be a good defense attorney, Maria. I just don't think my heart is in it," Everett said, hardly above a whisper. What a thing to say to his boss but fuck it. What did he have to lose at that point?

"I know your heart isn't in it," she said as she stroked his arm. "But you can't move up in this industry without getting some dirt on your knees." She smiled at him, and he turned his face toward her.

He forgot about the case for a moment as her dark eyes pried into his. Her striking, beautiful, dark eyes. *Does she want me to kiss her? I'm not kissing her. What if she doesn't want me to kiss her? Can you spell "sexual harassment"?*

Maria cleared her throat, eliminating the uncomfortable and heavy silence.

"Just trust yourself and keep those eyes open." She smiled and Everett's gaze became entrapped in the sight of her red lips. "And remember, find the vulnerability and exploit it."

Everett looked back out the window as her high-heeled steps receded behind him. His door eased shut, and he found himself missing her presence. Her friendship.

Dude, she's your boss.

"Way to blow it, Romeo," Renee said behind him.

He almost turned to face her, but he didn't want to get caught talking to air again. "What are you talking about?"

"I was here for the entire exchange. The way she looked at you . . . she wants you, Ev. That was your chance."

Everett shook his head and looked down at his feet. Shiny brown penny loafers looked back at him. He used to call them old-man shoes. When had he become such a stuffed shirt? "I don't know what you're talking about, Renee. Maria is my boss. She doesn't see me like that."

Her presence drew closer, bringing a breeze and a faint scent of gardenias with her. "So she never tried anything with you all these years?"

"No. Never."

"Perfect! That means she respected our marriage, which makes her exactly the sort of woman I want you to move on with."

"You're missing the whole she's-my-fucking-boss bit," he said with a sigh. "Even if she wanted me—which she certainly does not—we can't pursue anything because I'm her subordinate."

Renee clicked her tongue against the roof of her mouth, a habit she developed when deep in thought. "Then we've got to get you over to the other side of the fence. If you're on the prosecution's side, you could pursue her, right?"

"Maybe if my new boss is okay with it, but that still—"

"No more excuses. Let's find your golden case so any prosecutorial teams would be stupid to turn you down."

He had to turn his head and look at her now. Since when did she know such lawyerly words?

"What?" she said with a shrug. "I watched a lot of *Law & Order* while you were working late."

Everett walked to his desk and finally found the courage to look through the case file again. "Golden case," he whispered to himself. "I just need to find my golden case."

"And fall in love with Maria," Renee added.

"Get that one out of your transparent head," he said with his eyes still glued to the stack of cases. "I already got a woman who was out of my league once. I'll never be able to do that again."

When Renee didn't respond, he thought she'd vanished, but when he looked up, she still stood by the window. Her back was to him, her dark hair falling in waves over her slender shoulders. Finding the golden case was one thing, but he'd never find another golden woman like Renee.

CHAPTER TWELVE

E verett tried to use chopsticks to eat his takeout. He put the tips into the rice and willed his fingers to work the sticks properly. They crossed each other and were unable to pick up a thick piece of chicken, let alone a grain of rice. *Can I literally do anything?* He paused for a moment. *Actually, who the fuck even uses the chopsticks?* Everett tossed the sticks onto the table, sending a splatter of soy sauce across the case file.

"Shit!" he yelled as he dabbed at the paper with a napkin. He trudged to the kitchen and grabbed a fork, giving up on his attempt to be cultured and eat like a normal, sad American man. He plunged the fork into the chicken and rice and brought it to his mouth. After wiping his fingers on his sweatpants—because fuck a napkin—he turned to the next page in the Ortiz file.

"Murder." He read the charge again before fumbling through the file to pull out the autopsy report. His favorite thing to analyze because he knew fuck-all about anatomy. Might as well be in Spanish.

The victim is a 47-year-old Hispanic female.
Injuries sustained: (1) approximately 4cm laceration to the anterior
wall of the chest. Diffuse blood in the chest cavity.

Whoever took this woman out had a serious bone to pick with her. No wonder the cops pegged the husband for the job. This attack was personal.

Cause of death: Traumatic aortic rupture.

Everett sighed and picked up the evidence photos next. A clear bag with a knife took up the entire image. The crime scene photos followed behind it. Everett shuddered, put the photos down, and dropped his face into his hands.

"Yet another unwinnable case." He leaned over and closed the takeout container. Viewing those crime scene photos hadn't exactly bolstered his appetite.

Everett carried his leftovers to the fridge and plopped onto the couch in the living room. He flipped on the news and immediately regretted not taking his sorry ass straight to bed. His case was still headlining. *Great, the publicity makes it real easy to get a fair trial.*

He watched as his client's mugshot flashed across the screen. His eyes were cold and crazed, probably because he was fucking crazy. *From the way he looks, maybe we have a chance at an insanity plea.* Everett stared at the screen, trying to see the scene firsthand. The front of the home was cordoned off with yellow caution tape. Police lights strobed in the background. The officers were shown dragging his client out in a bathrobe, and he never looked up from the ground, transfixed on the concrete in front of him.

"Miguel Ortiz is a forty-five-year-old construction worker charged with the second-degree murder of his wife, Helena Ortiz. He is held without bail, pending trial."

"Jesus wept," Everett said to himself.

Everett picked up his phone and called Clarke, because who the hell else could he call about murder?

"Hello?" Clarke answered.

"Did you see my client on Channel 3 news?"

"Channel 3 and Channel 5, actually. That sure is getting a *lot* of media coverage."

"The news coverage is only going to make finding an unbiased jury even harder," Everett said as he dropped his head back against the couch.

"That neighborhood is bad news. It's the third murder this month there. That's probably why it's getting so much coverage."

"That's fantastic. Do you think I have a chance in hell at winning this case?"

There was a long hesitation. "I mean, there's always a chance, Everett."

"That's what I thought. Well, the boss lady thinks I have what it takes, but man, I sure don't think so." Everett sighed.

"I take it your talk with Maria went well?"

A vision of how she'd looked at him by the window bolted through his mind. Had she been giving him signals? Renee sure seemed to think so. "Hey, have you ever seen Maria date anyone from the office?"

"Doesn't-know-how-to-have-human-emotions Maria?"

"Yes, that's the one. She looked like she wanted me to kiss her today, but maybe I'm just losing my mind." Everett laughed.

"That would be one way to get better cases." Clarke chuckled. "She's so robotic, though. I don't think my dick could stay hard if I tried to sleep my way up *that* ladder."

"I'm not going to sleep my way up the ladder. And she's not robotic. She's focused. But I see why others would find it off-putting. We actually had a really nice talk on Friday. I told her my heart just wasn't in being a defense attorney."

Clarke gasped. "You said that? And she didn't fire you on the spot? I would have. You chose to begin your law career as a defense attorney. Now you want to jump ship?"

Everett was finding Clarke's tone pretty fucking hostile. "I became a defense attorney because I wanted to help people. I never realized just how few people are actually not guilty. It's all about how well you play the system to let murderers walk the streets again. I just can't keep doing it."

"You're overly sensitive. Ever since Renee—" Clarke stopped his sentence, which was wise.

"I know where you're going with that. I lost my wife for this job that I hate. And my happiness is on its last breath too. If I don't find a bit of purpose here soon, I'm going to go nuts."

"Well, get out while you still can. Otherwise, buckle up and enjoy our ride to hell."

"I'll try. I'll see you tomorrow," Everett said before hanging up the phone.

He clicked off the television. Scrubbing a hand down his face, he plodded to the bedroom and stripped down to his boxers before climbing into bed.

CHAPTER THIRTEEN

Several days had passed, and Everett hadn't seen Renee. Sitting at his desk in his office, Everett closed his eyes and willed her to appear. He gritted his teeth and concentrated harder, screaming her name in his mind. A knock at his door broke his concentration and sent his heart galloping out of his chest. He opened his eyes. Maria stood on the other side of the door, an awkward smile plastered on her beautiful face. Flames engulfed his cheeks as he waved her in.

Maria accentuated the movement of her hips as she entered Everett's office. He ran his hands through the mess of paperwork and manilla folders, searching through the battlefield of files for something to look at and think about other than his boss.

"Any luck with the Ortiz case?" Maria asked as she smoothed her skirt before sitting in one of the overstuffed leather chairs across from Everett. She crossed her legs.

"Nada. Nil. Zilch. The case is solid, and Prosecutor McNinch is a force to be reckoned with," Everett said as he idly shuffled the papers again. "I met with Miguel a few days ago, and of course he's crying innocence."

Maria leaned over and touched his hand. Their eyes met, and they stared at each other for much too long. Her full lips, painted in a deep shade of maroon, were slightly parted, and her deep brown eyes were rich like fine chocolate. "I have faith in you, Everett."

"At least one of us does," he said with a dry laugh as he closed the file and adjusted the top button on his suit. When had it gotten so hot in his office?

"The discovery hearing is . . ." Maria looked at the calendar on the wall and squinted her eyes. "Less than two weeks away. If you don't have anything solid by next week, I say we go to the hearing and hope for the best. Maybe someone will fuck up somewhere along the way." Maria smiled. She was trying to give him hope where there was none.

"Are you even allowed to talk to me like that?" Everett smiled back, turning up the dial on his flirtation a bit, but that was about as high as the dial could go.

Maria bit her lip. "You're right. I probably shouldn't say *fuck* around you." She said the word "fuck" slowly. Her top teeth pressed against her lower lip, hovering there for a teasing moment. He watched her mouth, adjusting his tie as he began to sweat.

"It's okay." He looked down at his paper and cursed to himself under his breath. *Make a move,* he thought as he tried to encourage himself to ask her out. He cleared his throat. "You wouldn't like to go to dinner, maybe? We could discuss the case." *Yeah, that was good. Use the pretense of work to seem less threatening.*

"Everett." Her lips pouted. "I can't have any type of relationship outside of work with my subordinates."

"No problem. Thought I'd ask," Everett said with a sigh. *I thought I was reading this situation better.*

"If anything ever changes, though, I would love to go to dinner." She smiled at him softly and stood to adjust her skirt. Everett noticed the top button undone on her shirt, exposing an intoxicating hint of her cleavage.

Maria swayed her hips as she turned to leave, her high heels tapping the tiles as she approached the door and left his office.

"You really are dense," Renee said beside him.

He turned his chair to face her, then remembered the prying eyes around his office space. Lifting a file from his desk, he leaned back in his chair and pretended to read aloud. "Where have you been? I thought you'd finally moved on."

Renee shrugged. "No such luck. I thought staying away might make it easier for you. Out of sight, out of mind. But after seeing this weak display, I realize you need my help more than ever."

"Weak display? I asked her to dinner," he said in a harsh whisper. "She turned me down."

"No, she said she couldn't date a subordinate. Remember when you told her you wanted to change teams?"

Everett nodded.

"You didn't find it odd that she wasn't supremely pissed about that?"

"Well, I mean, I just . . ."

"She wants you to change teams so she can explore something with you."

Everett closed his mouth and blinked. These were all very good points. "And she said if anything changes—"

"Exactly!" Renee moved closer and kneeled in front of him. "So how soon can you get a job with the other side?"

He ran his hand through his hair. "It's not that simple. I can't just walk into a law firm and get hired on, especially not at my current rate. I need to make them want me so they'll offer competitive pay, and that means winning a case."

"Then win a case?"

"Again, not that simple. Every case that comes across my desk is an unwinnable disaster." He closed the file in his hand and looked at the miniature clock on his desk. "It's quitting time and I need a break. Let's go home."

He tucked the Ortiz folder into his briefcase and shut off the lights.

THE TV BUZZED to life as Everett sat down with a game controller for the first time in months. *Some good ol' fashion me time,* he thought as he popped open a beer and turned on his gaming console. Renee hated when he played video games, so he didn't often play. The controller vibrated in greeting and his excitement rose.

Everett's thumbs moved wildly as his character climbed into a flashy car and proceeded to take out streetlights, other cars, and human beings. His body tilted as he made sudden turns in the car.

"This game is violent," Renee said as she appeared beside him. The light from the screen reflected in his eyes as she stared at it with a twist in her lip.

"It's fun," he told her without looking at her. His character hailed a prostitute, and they got into his dented car. The car rocked back and forth for a few seconds before the woman got out again and tried to walk away. "Tried" being the operative word. Everett's character rushed her with a bat and beat her to death before retrieving his money from her splayed corpse.

"Wow, is that how you feel about women?" Renee asked.

"No, not always." He chuckled. "Sometimes I just back into them after they get out if I'm feeling really lazy."

Renee rolled her eyes. "What are those stars in the corner?"

"Those are goals. The more stars you accumulate, the more cops come after you. Sometimes I steal the cop car and continue my carnage with my sirens on. Whoop, whoop!" He made a poor attempt at the sound of a police siren.

"This is stupid," Renee said, though she didn't look away. "Wait, now you're in a helicopter? Why would you steal a helicopter?"

"The real question is, why *wouldn't* you steal a helicopter?" A few minutes later, a fiery helicopter crash ended his rampage. "Fine, I'll play something less violent," he said as he went to the main menu and pulled up another game.

"Okay, you're a cowboy now. That doesn't seem so bad." Renee smiled.

Everett smirked as Renee's smile turned into a frown.

"That woman just asked you for a ride to town and you hog-tied her and threw her in a river!"

"Yes, I sure did."

"Rude." Renee's lips tightened. "Pull her out before she drowns."

Everett did as she suggested . . . and dropped her onto the nearby train tracks just as a whistling locomotive crested the hill.

"Oh, the guy with the snakebite! Are you going to suck the venom out?"

"No, fuck that guy. I already sucked him twice now. Dude needs to stay out of the woods. I don't have time for that shit. I have killin' and robbin' to do." Everett took a long sip of beer. He was enjoying getting in touch with his childish side for once.

"Did you just say robbin'?"

"Sure did."

"Oh, look at that cute farm!"

Renee watched in horror as Everett stampeded around the farm, killing and skinning every animal he found—the cows, the pigs, and even the chickens.

"Don't worry, they'll respawn. Then I can do it all over again. Now I have enough meat to give my character the same attractive physique as me." He patted his belly and laughed.

"Don't you have something else you could be doing besides wasting time on video games? Isn't there a case you're supposed to be working on?" Her voice was laced with judgment, and it irked him. He thought he'd escaped that part of marriage. The nagging.

"Of course, but I want to have some me time, unbothered." He glared at her. "I don't care if you hang out, but stop trying to control me. You lost that privilege when you chose to leave me. Forgive me if I want to forget about my life for a few hours."

"Jogging helped me—"

Everett interrupted her with a harsh glare.

"Sorry. Forget it." Her form landed beside him on the couch. "I just want this to end. I want you to find happiness so I can be dead. Like, really dead."

He paused the game and dropped the controller onto the coffee table. "Maybe we should explore other avenues. Switching to the prosecution's side could take a while, and I can't pursue Maria until then."

"What about that dating app? Did you ever finish filling it out?"

Everett nodded. "Yeah, but that's not what I mean. We shouldn't put all of our scrambled eggs into one busted basket. I still think we should explore the reason why you killed yourself. You probably have unfinished business."

Renee shook her head. "No, that's not it."

"How do you know? Maybe a medium could help."

"No."

Everett threw his arms in the air. "Why not? I've been trying your way and it's not working! We should try both ways at the same time." He lifted his beer, but it was empty.

"I don't have anything to hide, Everett. I don't know why I killed myself, but it's not important." The look in her eyes said otherwise. "I'm really tired now. I think I need to go back to my white room and recharge."

As she dissipated beside him, his stomach dropped. Renee was hiding something.

CHAPTER FOURTEEN

E verett clicked the heart at the bottom of nearly every profile that popped up within fifty miles. Not many returned the interest. He had a message from a woman nearby, but her profile showed her surrounded by six dogs. Six *tiny* dogs that probably bit ankles and barked whenever the wind blew near their assholes the wrong way. He deleted the message and was about to close his laptop when a new alert informed him someone had liked his profile. He clicked the link.

A busty blonde stared back at him from the screen, her wet cleavage pushed nearly to her chin. A skimpy white bikini covered little more than her nipples—which poked against the thin fabric. Shimmering ocean water obscured her lower half, but if her toned arms were any indication, her stomach would be as flat as a soda left in the summer sun.

His fingers moved over the keyboard, frantically typing a message before the blonde—screen name LovelyKiss227—could change her mind.

"It's a catfish," Renee said.

Everett looked up at her with his eyebrows pulled together.

"A catfish is someone who makes a fake profile to hook you in. Did you even read her bio?"

Everett's fingers stopped flying. He opened a second tab and navigated to her profile. A paragraph filled with broken English stared back at him, dropping his stomach to his feet.

"I enjoy long walk on beach," Renee said through a laugh. "We talk much soon . . . for good times!"

"Maybe she's from another country," he said, brushing off her giggles. He clicked back to his message and continued typing. "I won't fault the woman for her lack of linguistic skills. If she's escaped the horrors of a third-world country, it would be cruel to toss her aside for that."

Renee flicked her wrist in the air and shook her head. "Okay, but when she starts asking for money, don't say I didn't warn you."

With a grumble, he deleted the message and clicked through more profiles. A dark-haired woman flashed onto the screen, her features eerily similar to Renee's—the same dark waves of hair, dark eyes, and perfect pout, though her nose was a bit thinner. His finger hovered over his touchpad, tempted to move to the next woman to avoid any hare-brained ideas of having sex with someone who *looked* like his should-have-been-dearly-departed wife. But he couldn't do it. He clicked the heart instead.

Raggedy trumpets played a sad fanfare through the laptop speakers, and a white banner flew across the screen. It's a Match! the banner read. Before he had a chance to send her a message, a chat bubble popped into the bottom right corner.

FlyingFree777: Hey, cute picture!
EvEnders69: Thanks, it's my bathroom.

He wanted to bury his head in the sand and never resurface. As if she couldn't tell it was his bathroom from the fucking sink in the center of the picture.

FlyingFree777: Well, it's very nice. You don't have a girlfriend or anything do you?
EvEnders69: No, I'm very single. Why do you ask?
FlyingFree777: I don't know many men who use a skin care line XD

He looked at his profile picture again. Renee's entire army of skin care products dominated the shelf on the wall behind him. He didn't want to run her off by bringing up his dead wife, so he moved past it. He could explain later—if he made it to later.

EvEnders69: Would you want to grab a coffee some time? I'll teach you all my skin care secrets.
FlyingFree777: This app isn't for coffee dates ;)
EvEnders69: What are you asking?

What *was* she asking? He'd been out of the dating game for so long that he had no clue what women wanted any longer. He felt like he was in another damn universe. What happened to buying a woman a drink from the bar? Now people searched for dates without even putting on pants. Another message popped onto the screen.

FlyingFree777: Netflix and chill or . . .
EvEnders69: Oh, well, yeah. That's cool too. Tonight?

Everett reread his messages and slapped his head with his hand. He'd be surprised if she responded. He was bringing the 2000s back, one date at a time.

FlyingFree777: It's a date! I'm Megan, by the way.
EvEnders69: I'm Everett. See you tonight.

EVERETT SMILED in the mirror as he slid his arms into his gray dress shirt. He buttoned it up all the way, doing a half circle in the mirror to see how he looked. *Oof.* He finally decided on buttoning it up halfway, which was a viable compromise; he could keep his stomach concealed while still looking aloof. His soft, dark chest hair poked out from the splayed collar. He picked up a bottle of cologne and spritzed it on both sides of his neck. The masculine aroma of sandalwood and leather soothed his frayed nerves. It had been a long time since he wore that scent. Renee used to say how much she loved it. Everett brushed back his brown hair and checked his style one final time. Before he could change anything for a third time, the doorbell rang.

As he shuffled to the door, a light sweat popped onto his brow. *Sweat? Did I remember deodorant?* He rushed back to the bathroom, undid a few buttons, and crammed the stick of Old Spice into his pits. His fingers shook as he fastened the buttons again and bolted to the door.

The dark-haired beauty stood on his doorstep. The woman had Renee's soft, feminine features, and it made him clear his throat nervously at the sight of her. A snug strapless dress in a bewitching shade of red hugged her like a second skin and stopped high on her toned thighs. Her bare shoulders caught the porch light, her skin glowing with each movement. She looked so soft.

"Megan?" Everett asked with a smile.

The woman nodded and Everett stepped aside to let her in. He offered a handshake, cursing himself for seeming like such an old man. He tried to play it off by going in for an even more awkward half-hug.

"I'm Everett. Lovely to meet you. Sorry to stare, but you remind me so much of someone." Everett looked down at the table by the door. A photo of Renee smiled up at him. He snatched the frame onto its face under the disguise of accidentally knocking into the table.

"Hopefully someone good!" She chuckled as she slipped her heels off at the door.

Thank god. Everett hated outside shoes inside the house. He cringed at the thought of all the bacteria and dirt and street crud the sole of a shoe could carry.

He led her into the living room and sat beside her on the sofa. He'd already cued up Netflix and had a bowl of popcorn on the table. Megan eyed the set-up.

With a flirty gaze, she looked back at Everett. "We don't actually have to watch Netflix, you know. I'm fine with just the *chill*." She dropped her mouth open, accentuating her full lips.

The glow from the TV illuminated the dark room just enough. In that light, Everett could almost pretend he was with Renee again, which was really fucking creepy for everyone involved.

"Don't you want to know anything about me?" Everett asked. "Maybe what I do for work or—"

Megan interrupted him with an aggressive kiss, her hands wandering toward his lap. "I don't really care, if you want me to be honest. I just care about one thing right now." Her hand pressed against the front of his pants.

Everett pulled his face away from her mouth. "Tell me about yourself?" he asked through her oblivious advances. Discomfort radiated from every pore on his body like he was a damn virgin. Actually, he was pretty sure virgins had better sexual energy.

"We can talk after." She grabbed his face and pulled him in for another kiss. "Maybe." She smirked as she snagged his lower lip between her teeth and straddled his lap.

He'd tried to be respectful, but this woman wanted none of it. She only desired what he had between his legs, and who was he to argue with a woman who knew what she wanted? When his shoulders relaxed, her hungry hands ripped apart his shirt and clawed at the zipper of his pants. Her animalistic groans and grunts equally turned him on and terrified him.

"Let me get a condom." Everett tried to slide from beneath her, but her body was immovable. Or maybe he didn't try quite hard enough. He lost his sanity for a moment as he kissed her and stripped his shirt off his arms, tossing it to the floor. His hands raced along her sides and grabbed her ass. *I still got it*, he thought. With nothing between them but a raised skirt and her panties, he felt the warm heat of her. She reached down, pulled her underwear aside, and lowered his boxers. Her hand wrapped around the base of his dick to help guide him inside her.

"Are you fucking crazy, Everett?" Renee screeched from beside him.

Everett pulled his cock away and motioned to Megan to wait by putting his hands together in a T shape, requesting a time out.

"Were you just going to fuck this stranger with no condom?" Renee's voice rose with sharp surprise. "You, Everett, the one who won't even touch a doorknob with your bare hand? Her crotch is like . . . the dirtiest doorknob."

Everett laughed nervously as the woman glared at him. Renee was right. He used his sleeve to open doors and push buttons. The only place he let his hands get a little dirty was at the strip club, and even then, he carried hand sanitizer in his breast pocket. He learned real quick not to use it in front of the dancers.

"I can't do this," Everett said as he pulled up his boxers. "I'm . . ." Everett looked around for an excuse that wouldn't hurt the girl's feelings. He stared at Renee. "I'm married! I'm married, and this guilt just really got to me. Curse this conscience of mine!" He lifted his balled fists in feigned frustration.

Megan drew her hand back, smacked him, and climbed off his lap. "Asshole!" she yelled. "You said you were single!"

He dropped his head back as he heard her heels on the laminate floor before she opened and slammed the door behind her.

"I thought this was what you wanted," Everett whimpered.

Renee folded her arms over her chest. "When I said get back on the horse, I didn't mean for you to bareback the first one that let you ride her."

"Oh god, what was I thinking?" Everett said as he put his hand on his crotch. "I just lost control and all sense of myself. She looked so much like you, I could almost pretend she *was* you."

Renee straddled Everett's lap, which made him jump. She wasn't real matter anymore, so he couldn't feel her weight on his lap, but somehow, he could still feel *her*.

He looked up at her, and the memories of times she'd straddled him this same way rushed to the front of his mind. The way her beautiful, long eyelashes reached toward the sky, the soft curve of her nose, and her pouting lips—he remembered them all from this angle. He remembered devouring her skin, the way the light salt of it electrified the tip of his tongue. Everett lifted his hands and let them slide down what would have been Renee's sides. She closed her eyes, as if remembering his touch as well.

"I can almost feel you," she whispered, a tear slipping down her cheek.

"I think I need a therapist." He laughed and dropped his head back. "What I wouldn't give to have you again, Renee. I can't stop asking why this happened." His lower lip quivered at the question.

"I don't know," Renee said with a drop of her gaze. Everett stared at the eyelashes encasing her beautiful eyes. "I really don't remember."

She had to remember. What was she keeping from him? She could tell him anything. Everything was fixable. Everything except her death.

CHAPTER FIFTEEN

W hy was this so damn complicated? On top of grocery shopping—which he'd never done without Renee's assistance—he had to bring a dish to the yearly Enders' family cookout. Everett put his hand on his chin and tried to figure out why there were so many different fruits and vegetables and what the fuck he was supposed to do with them. It was fucking magic how Renee would take those random raw foods and turn them into something magnificent.

He picked up a spiky pink fruit, cocking his head at it. *Dragon fruit. What the hell do you do with this?* It looked like something made up, conjured in the mind of a person who had never seen a fruit before. He sighed, put the odd thing down, and lifted a tiny fruit about the size of an olive that he mistook for little oranges. He bent down to look at the tag. *Kumquat.* For fuck's sake. He knew grapes, and even then, they had grapes that were flavored like cotton candy. *America.* Even the rack of apples overwhelmed him. Different colors, different names. He just wanted a normal fucking apple, the kind Renee used to get him.

"You like honeycrisp," Renee said as she popped up beside him. Everett jumped, knocking into the racks of apples. He reached out to catch them as they began a hurried descent toward the ground, but it was no use. He ended up with three in his arms and about forty-five around his feet. A store employee put his hands on his hips and stared at him.

"Forget the damn apples," he grumbled as he tried to pick them up, putting them in the wrong racks and bruising their red skins. "This is why you wash them, Renee."

Renee chuckled. She never washed apples. After a quick rub on her shirt, she'd take a careless bite. Pesticides, bacteria, and dirt from the damn floor—she just ate all of it. Everett washed the hell out of them.

Everett grabbed a tomato and tossed it into the cart.

"Might want to look at that one," she said in an even tone.

He picked it up and looked at it. A circular soft spot darkened the skin, and tiny white insects wiggled and squirmed through the pulpy mush. *Oh god.* "Forget the damn tomatoes too."

"Are you just going to live off Pop-Tarts?"

Everett groaned and headed toward the deli. The man behind the counter turned toward him. A wiry white mustache danced just below his nose, the perfect accessory to his mostly white butcher's jacket. Everett tried to keep his eyes away from the brown stains decorating it here and there.

"What can I get you?"

Everett's eyes widened as he saw seven different hunks of turkey. He looked at the man with a pleading expression before he turned to face Renee. But she was gone. *Great.*

"I . . . don't . . . know," Everett stammered. "My wife used to do all the shopping."

"Well, there's oven-roasted, low-sodium oven-roasted . . . actually there's two brands of oven-roasted. There's smoked, mesquite-smoked, and honey-smoked."

Everett wanted to vomit. Why was there so much goddamn turkey? Turkey. The kind Renee got. That's all he wanted. He pointed to the mesquite-smoked hunk of meat. The man nodded and pulled it from the case.

"Thin, medium, or thick sliced? Do you want half a pound, a whole pound?"

Everett rubbed the bridge of his nose. "Can you show me the difference?"

The man beside the meat shaver rolled his eyes. He adjusted a setting and rubbed the meat across the metal. "Thick." He held it up for Everett to examine.

"Can I touch it?" Everett asked.

A woman beside him gave him a dirty look. The butcher held the slice over the counter and tossed it into his hand. The thickness was good, but the color wasn't right. The edges were covered in too many spices. The turkey he was used to was boring.

"I think . . . it's the oven-roasted turkey after all."

The man behind the counter groaned, and murmurs rolled over the crowd gathering behind him in line. His face flushed with heat. The butcher grabbed the oven-roasted turkey, but Everett noticed his flesh popping through a hole in his glove as he set it on the shaver. *Oh god.* He watched as he rubbed his bare finger along the meat, touching it everywhere as he spun it around on the machine.

Everett sighed. "Never mind, I don't want any turkey," he said with a hurried breath. He ran off before the crowd behind him could come at him with pitchforks.

As he rushed past the deli section, he grabbed a tub of pre-made potato salad. It was better than nothing, and it was the best he could do.

FROM THE MOMENT Everett stepped out of the car, he could smell the scent of barbecue rising from a charcoal grill in the corner of the park. As the grass brushed his ankles, he cursed himself for wearing shorts. The lush green blades struck his skin with every step, and he reached down and scratched the forming itch as he swatted away mosquitoes.

"God, I hate the outdoors."

His family absorbed him as he reached the pavilion. Long-distance aunts and uncles and cousins that he didn't care for hugged him as if he ever mattered to them. Everyone kept apologizing for his loss, and the uncomfortable amount of sympathy pouring from people he didn't even like made him feel sick. The only person who didn't swarm him was his Aunt Marlo. Instead of acknowledging him and his loss, she sat at a picnic table, swigging alcohol from a flask like her life depended on it.

That's a mood I can empathize with, Everett thought with a laugh.

He made his way through the thick throng of people and sat across from her. He didn't speak, and her glossy eyes made him wonder if she would either. He wished he could be half as drunk as she was right about then.

"Sorry about your wife. Sucks." She slurred her words as she twisted the cap off the small metal flask with one hand and leaned her head back for another sip.

"Sorry about your liver," Everett quipped.

"Ah, piss on it. You gotta die from something, and with any luck, my demise will involve alcohol."

Renee appeared beside Everett with a scrunched face. "Where am I?" she asked with panic rising in her voice. "Oh god, no. This isn't the family function I tactfully miss every year, is it?" She looked around at his mom and dad and all their extended family. Everett gave her a sideways glance.

"What's been going on with the fam?" he asked his soused aunt.

"Well, two of your aunts are estranged. They've claimed opposite sides of the pavilion and are defending their areas like a turf war." She laughed as she gestured toward one aunt with a chair pulled to the very end of the left side of the pavilion, and his other aunt on the right. "It's like The Punks versus The Warriors over here."

"What was the fight about?"

"That piece of shit house our parents left us. They left it to *me* even though I told them I didn't want fuck all to do with that dump. The thing would be worth more if we accidentally burned it down on purpose. Anyway, I told my sisters they have to fight for it, and whoever kills the other first, wins. Neither of them is happy with that, so they're mad at me *and* each other. Shit, I'm good at tearing the whole family apart." She smirked.

"I don't mind *her*." Renee looked around. "Oh god, is that your uncle?"

Everett followed her gaze and spotted Uncle Randall, shirtless, drinking beer, and eating hot dogs as he cooked on the grill. The ketchup fell from the bun and dripped down his round, hairy stomach. As he bent to retrieve a fresh beer from the cooler, his half-eaten hotdog fell off his plate and rolled across the concrete. Without missing a beat, Uncle Randall lifted the grit-covered bun, blew on it, and put it back on the plate. *Unhygienic.* A shudder worked its way through Everett's body. Everything about that half of his family was a walking *E. coli* outbreak waiting to happen.

He made his way across the lawn to get a hamburger, something he hadn't seen hit the ground yet. His drunk uncle nodded in recognition, lifted a burger off the grill, and dropped it on a cheap, too-small bun.

"Sorry about your wife." He coughed and scratched at his belly. "You know the saying, though. Plenty of pussy in the sea."

"That's not an actual saying." Everett pursed his lips and took the burger back to the picnic table. Red-tinged grease leaked from it, and his stomach twisted. He took a bite, looked within the burger, and regretted having eyeballs almost immediately. Raw meat stared back at him. It would probably run off with a *moo* as he spat it on the ground beside him.

"Is there a particular reason we're letting the alcoholics be the gatekeepers for preventing foodborne illnesses?" He tried to rinse the taste out of his mouth with water.

His aunt gestured toward her flask. He took a quick swig and coughed. The liquor was so strong he was sure nothing bacterial could survive anything it touched. Renee laughed at his misfortune.

"Can I have that burger?" a kid with a spiked helmet asked Everett.

"No, Raymond, you can't. It's not cooked," Everett told him.

"Can I have it *please*?" he begged with pouty lips.

"Go get one over there." Everett pointed toward the grill.

"I don't want one of those. I want this one."

Aunt Marlo unburied her head from her arm cocoon and sat up with squinted eyes. With a groan, she pushed the plate toward the kid. "Now fuck off," she said and waved him away.

The kid snatched the plate with greedy fingers and ran off.

"Marlo . . ."

She shrugged. "He's a kid. Kids are resilient. Besides, I've watched that kid eat worse."

Everett's mom started toward them, and Renee, Everett, and Aunt Marlo cursed under their breath in unison. Renee sat taller and Everett tried to curl into a ball, hoping she wouldn't notice him. There'd been very little interaction since the whole your-wife-was-a-whore conversation went down.

"Hi, Marlo. I see you're drinking," his mom said. Marlo raised her flask and smiled. His mom turned her gaze onto him. "You know, Renee never even met the rest of your family. She always acted so much better than us."

"Mom, your brother is burning his belly hairs and spreading foodborne illness, your other two sisters are yelling at each other from across the pavilion as they attempt to recruit family members to their sides, and I'm fairly certain my little cousin over there is licking an anthill. We have a pretty low bar."

His mom sucked her teeth. "It doesn't matter. She should have had the decency to make an appearance."

Renee had done anything she could to avoid these get-togethers, and now he understood why. She would fake being sick or pretend she needed to be at her own family obligations. She'd even picked up a part-time job a week before the event *just* so she had an excuse to get out of it.

Renee walked over to his cousin and squatted down. The kid looked up, lapping at the dirt circling his mouth. Ants scattered for their lives, racing off in every direction around his grimy sneakers.

"Dude, that kid is actually licking an anthill!" Renee shouted. "I don't think your hamburger is going to be a problem!" The kid stared at her, almost as if he could see her. She waved her hand in front of his face, and his eyes followed her. "Holy shit, I think this kid can see me. It's like the lights are on, but no one's home." She put her hand back down at her side.

The child's mom came over and grabbed his hand. "I told you to stop eating weird stuff, Raymond. Do you want worms again?"

Renee tightened her lips and walked back to Everett. "Your family is fucking strange. Tip to tail. The weird apple fell from the weird tree and hit every branch on the way down. How are you so normal?" Renee put her hand to her chin, rubbing it for a moment. "Well, normal*ish*."

"Where's Roman?" Everett asked his mom.

She shrugged. "Couldn't make it, I guess. He probably—"

Before she could finish her sentence, a loud muscle car pulled into the parking lot. Roman stepped out and brushed his hair back as he walked toward them. He looked so fit in a tight athletic shirt and basketball shorts. His muscles rippled under the fabric, causing Everett to feel even more insecure about his flab. He hated these barbecues because everyone fawned over Roman from the moment he arrived. Even the two feuding aunts inched a little closer to the group congregating around him.

"Hey, family people." Roman hugged everyone but Everett. In fact, he hardly looked at him at all.

"Whose car is that?" someone asked.

Roman puffed his overly large chest. "A client's. Bigwig. He said I could take it for a spin after I finished working on it."

Roman was a car detailer, though he liked to make it sound like he was a mechanic. He took vacations so often because he had no girlfriend and zero obligations. It would make Everett anxious to be that willy-nilly with his money and time.

Everett looked at the uncle with a dried ketchup stain on his belly, his aunt passed out on the picnic table, and his little cousin picking dandelions and aggressively biting off the flowers. They weren't a classy family, and Roman always put on airs as if he weren't one of them. But he most definitely was. He was just good at hiding it.

"He sure is a cocky son of a bitch, isn't he?" Renee mumbled.

"The cockiest," Everett responded with a sigh.

"Technically, you have the best job here," Renee said, "and I don't see you bragging about it."

"Yeah, because I try not to remind them I'm a lawyer. Pretty much every holiday or event involves someone asking me how to get out of their DUI, public indecency, or drug charge. My family is full of criminals," he said with a dry laugh. He got to his feet and strolled to a tree a little ways away from the pavilion. "You were right to avoid these things," he muttered.

"No, I should have come with you to support you," she said.

Everett smiled.

"What's so funny?" Renee asked.

He shook his head and looked at his feet. "Just that it took your death for us to realize all the ways we could have been better partners for each other. Because it would have been nice to have you here. Roman has outshined me in so many ways, but a beautiful, intelligent, witty woman chose me instead of him. And I took it for granted."

He looked up and met her eyes. Her lower lip quivered, and a well of tears built against her eyes until they spilled down her cheeks. "I'm sorry I did this to us."

"You still talking to your dead wife?" Roman said behind him. He'd been so caught up in his moment with Renee, he hadn't heard his brother approach.

"Nope, just talking to myself." He didn't want to give Roman any more ammo against him.

"That's still seen as crazy in most circles, bro." He clapped a massive hand on Everett's shoulder and attempted a pensive look. "I really think you need some help. Renee was nice enough, but was she worth all this torment?"

Everett's eyes went wide. Heat flamed into his cheeks, and his hand coiled into a tight fist. He wanted to stand up to his brother, wanted to tell him exactly what he thought of him. But he couldn't. Without another word, he stormed to his car and left the barbecue without saying goodbye, silently vowing to take a page from Renee's handbook and avoid these barbecues—and his asinine family—in the future. Only his drunken Aunt Marlo would be missed.

CHAPTER SIXTEEN

E verett pulled up in front of a small brick building. The faded red awning above the front door said Medium Well. All this time he thought it was a burger place he just never had a chance to check out. Visiting a psychic wasn't how he'd ever envisioned spending a Sunday, but he'd already wasted his Saturday at the family barbecue, so now seemed like as good a time as any.

Everett pulled the keys from the ignition and stepped out. He put his hands on top of his car, trying to figure out if he *really* planned to do this. Renee had seemed hellbent on avoiding psychic mediums, but what she didn't know wouldn't hurt her, and he hadn't seen her since the barbecue. The heat from the sun radiated off the roof, warming his hands. Everett stared at the building as a white-haired woman left the shop with a cat strapped to her chest like a baby.

What am I doing?

The bell dinged overhead when Everett opened the door. The sharp scent of incense infiltrated his nostrils with every breath he inhaled, though it wasn't quite strong enough to overpower the skunky aroma of pot smoke. A cream leather sofa with butt marks rubbed into the sunken cushions pressed against the window. He hoped he wasn't expected to sit there.

A woman appeared from the back room, parting a curtain of stringed beads as she entered. Her stringy brown hair fell down to her chest, and a gemstone hair piece wrapped around her head. Ebony eyeliner rimmed her brown eyes in thick strokes. The mascara caked to her sparse eyelashes gave them the appearance of hairy spider legs poking from her wrinkled lids. The various green gems and metal pieces hanging from her flowing white gown dangled and clinked against each other, singing a tune as she walked. She looked like the product of an unplanned mating between a hippie and an emo wannabe.

"Everett?" she asked with a smile.

Everett pointed to his chest. "How'd you know?"

"I'm a psychic, remember?" She giggled. "Actually, we don't get very many men as clients, so I remembered your name from our phone call a few days ago when you asked for directions." She smiled and Everett's posture deflated a bit. "Follow me to my room."

The brief moment of belief washed away when he realized how stupid he was being. This wasn't who he was. He relied on facts, not fantasy. Then again, having your dead wife appear before you on an almost daily basis was pretty out there.

The woman turned and pressed her fingers against crystals glued to the sides of the door frame—ocean-blue apatite, the cloudy blue-sky coloration of kyanite, and the purple hue of tanzanite. He only knew their names because of the labels beneath each stone. A small placard above them also touted their knack for unlocking and bolstering psychic abilities. They didn't seem to do enough, however, since she failed to realize how much he wanted to sink into the floor right then.

The woman guided Everett through the curtain of beads. The strands clapped together as they walked through, getting hung up on Everett's belt. He tugged down one of them by mistake, and it followed him to his seat like a string of cans tied to a groom's car. Soft zither music played in the background as the woman sat down at a round wooden table. She motioned for Everett to sit across from her, and he struggled to free the beaded string from his belt before he sat.

Various stones and crystals cluttered the table, and he found himself disappointed that she didn't glimpse the great beyond through a crystal ball like he'd seen on TV. A moth-eaten cloth lay beneath the array of mystical artifacts. It might have once been white, but years of use had left it yellowed and disgusting.

"It's one hundred dollars per session. Cash preferred." She smiled as she shuffled a deck of tarot cards. Her long purple nails caught the dim light with each movement. "I can do a discount if you want to add a chakra bundle to any service. I can also give you future readings and even read your past lives."

Past lives? What a scam. Everett hesitated for a moment before pulling out his wallet. "I just want to communicate with a deceased loved one. I need to know why they . . . did something before they passed." He chose his words carefully. If her abilities were genuine, she'd know the rest.

The moment the bill touched the table, the woman began to close her eyes, fluttering her lids as if she were possessed. Her chest gyrated and her nostrils flared with each exaggerated intake of breath. "I feel such a strong presence in this room." She opened her eyes and stared at Everett. "It's male . . ." She cocked her head at his lack of response. Her eyes fluttered again. "Actually, it's a female."

"Yes," Everett said.

She stopped for a moment and removed the money, sliding the bill into some unseen area below the table in one discreet motion. "This loss was very recent, and her presence is very pained."

His ears perked up, and he fought the urge to lean forward in his seat.

"I see her! She has hair that's this long." The woman started her hand horizontally at her chest and slowly moved up as she stared intensely at him.

"Yeah," Everett said as he stopped her, just about shoulder-length.

"She's a blonde. Yes, definitely a blonde."

"Not since 2012," Renee said with a smirk as she appeared behind the woman. "I told you this was a silly idea."

"Her hair is dark," Everett said, ignoring Renee—the dead person he could literally see and talk to without forking over one hundred dollars.

"You're right. The light behind her was so bright I thought she was blonde!" the woman exclaimed. "She's surrounded by a blinding white light, you see."

Renee mockingly looked around for any bright light. Everett wanted to wave her off, but the last thing he desired was to appear psychotic. Though, considering his current company, he'd probably fit right in.

The woman rubbed the fingers of each hand together as if she were rolling a grain of sand against her skin. "Is there something you'd like to tell her? Speak to her through me."

Everett hesitated. "I miss you," he said after clearing his throat.

"Miss me? You see me every day," Renee said.

"Yes, yes. She says she misses you as well," the woman said with an emphatic nod.

Renee rolled her eyes.

"Did you meet somewhere holy? A church, maybe?" the psychic asked.

"I mean, one of the girls danced in a slutty nun outfit sometimes," Renee said with a shrug.

"Absolutely not," Everett said, fighting back a laugh. "We met in a strip club, actually. It was a pretty unholy place."

The psychic blew the hair off her forehead and began to frantically organize her crystals. Her lips drew down in a tight line as she pivoted the reading.

"I see water. Did she pass in the water?"

Everett looked down at his lap before responding. "Yes."

"A boating accident? Or drowning?"

"No," Everett said. With every step forward the woman took, she immediately stumbled backward three more in the next breath. "We've never been on a boat."

"How did she pass?" the woman asked as she stroked a pink gemstone.

"Suicide," Everett whispered.

"*Oh*, I felt that. I can feel the pain and sadness she felt. It clearly was a suicide now," the woman said.

You thought we were drowning on a goddamn yacht, but okay.

"She harbors a secret that keeps her trapped in limbo." Renee and Everett both snapped their attention to the medium. She wrapped a gemstone in her hand and clutched it to her chest, panting as if she'd run a marathon in some other realm.

"She does?" Everett asked. He leaned in. "What kind of secret?"

Renee folded her arms over her chest and walked closer to

him. "You can't seriously believe her now, Everett. She's been wrong about everything else."

Everett shrugged off Renee, his eyes glued to the woman in front of him. "What do you see?"

The woman closed her eyes and pursed her lips. "Oof, well, that's some family drama I'd rather not get into." The woman shuddered and folded her hands in her lap.

Renee's leg shook beneath her slip. "This woman is a quack," she snapped.

"She's gone," the woman said as she dropped her head and closed her eyes. "It's a bit dangerous to keep going, but for the right price . . . I might be able to call her back."

"See!" Renee flung her hands toward the medium. "She just wants your money!"

Everett stood and pushed his chair under the table. "Thank you, this was really . . . insightful." In truth, he didn't know what to believe. She'd gotten most things wrong, but the way Renee reacted created more questions in his mind than answers. He walked out of the shop, once again tangling himself in the beads on his way out.

"I can do a love reading for another twenty-five dollars!" the medium called from behind him.

His jaw clenched. *Who do I believe? This woman is a quack. But what if there's some truth to the reading? What if some secret is keeping Renee trapped here?* It wasn't enough fuel to propel him back into the psychic's lair, however. He left the brick building and climbed into his car.

"ARE WE GOING to talk about what happened?" Renee asked as she paced behind him in the kitchen. Everett didn't answer as he scrubbed a plate in the sink. "Hello!" Renee tapped on his shoulder, but she couldn't touch him, and he couldn't feel her.

He slammed the plate into the drying rack, and it clinked against the metal. After drying his hands, he turned around, running into Renee directly behind him. "What is there to talk about?"

"You're behaving differently since you went to see that medium, if you can even call her that." She sucked her teeth. "You're clearly questioning everything about me, my character, and our relationship now."

Everett marched to the kitchen table and opened his laptop, turning it so Renee could read the screen. "When I got home, I researched why loved ones sometimes have trouble crossing over. Lies, secrets, and unfinished business are at the top of the list. I think there was a little bit of rightness within her wrongness." Everett met her eyes. "I wish you'd be honest with me."

Renee's lips tightened as her gaze went from him to the screen.

He was almost convinced she knew why this was happening. Deep in her unbeating heart, she knew what tethered her to the world of the living. So why couldn't she just tell him and move on? Unless she didn't want to move on . . . "No matter what it is, even if it breaks my heart, it has to be better than being stuck in this purgatory. Just tell—"

"Everett, I don't know why I'm stuck here! I don't know what unfinished business I have, besides the next fifty years of my life that I threw away! You're reading a bunch of hogwash and superstitions. No one actually knows how the spirit world works. Including me, and I'm fucking stuck here. And definitely not that woman you paid to 'read' me. With my luck, my unfinished business is forgetting to get your mom a present for her birthday a few months ago!" Renee threw her hands in the air.

"There's nothing you have done that I wouldn't forgive you for. I just want you to be at peace, and I want to move forward with my life," Everett said as he pulled out a chair and sat at the table.

"That's what I want too."

"It doesn't seem like it. I've tried doing it your way, but it's not working. It's time to try my way, and that means figuring out why you did this."

"I want you to move on, Everett, but not how you almost did with that woman the other night. Don't put yourself at risk to gain that forward momentum. Not only do you have to be mindful of catching something, but worse—and a lot more permanent—she could get knocked up."

"I know, Mother. I don't need a sex education class from a ghost." He looked up at Renee. The corners of her lips pulled down in a deep frown. "I'm sorry. I didn't mean it like that."

"I'm just trying to look out for you. She reminded you of me, and that was all it took. Had I not shown up, you'd have been balls deep in someone you don't even know. I don't give a flying fuck who you have sex with, but I won't sit back and let you make a mistake."

"It's not your place to interfere with my life anymore, Renee! I'm allowed to make mistakes. I'm a grown man. You've brought nothing but hurt to me since you've come back. You don't even see it! You've put a wedge between my brother and me, and you cock block me any chance you get!"

"A wedge between you and Roman?" Renee asked.

"I tried to tell him I could see you, and now he thinks I'm mental, so, yeah, he's not really beating down my door to hang out right now. He thinks I need a damn therapist."

"Well . . ."

"No. I don't need a therapist. I just need my shitty, sad life to be normal instead of shitty, sad, and haunted." As he glared at Renee, the coffee timer rang out, breaking the thick tension between them. He stood, opened the cabinet, and reached for his blue mug, bypassing the one in front with their faces on it. He filled it with fresh coffee, the steam rising up and the aroma infiltrating his senses. Renee stared at him, eyes narrowed as she disappeared before his very eyes.

CHAPTER SEVENTEEN

E verett looked at the clock on the wall and opened his mouth in a yawn. *Shit, it's after eight,* he thought with a heavy sigh. Time always got away from him. He swiveled around in the chair and looked at the nightlife bustling along the sidewalk below his office building. Headlights merged with streetlights and reflected up at him. Drunk girls giggled and swayed on skyscraper heels, stumbling with every step. *It's a fucking Monday night.* Everett was never like that in college. He was *boring*.

He turned back toward his desk and thumbed through the Ortiz file one more time. Brushing his hand through his hair, he released another wide yawn. This would not be his golden case. By the time the trial came, it would probably resemble petrified wood more than any precious metal.

"These late nights are what caused us problems in the first place," Renee said as she appeared in his office.

"I know, Renee, I know. I can't help it. This shitty case is driving me mad."

"Let me take a peek." She walked around Everett's desk and looked down at the file. "Spread the papers out."

Everett obliged and laid out each document from the file so she could read every line and peruse every image. He'd never done this while she was alive—major breach of the confidentiality code—but who could she tell now? Renee leaned over the desk and studied the first page, which detailed the defendant's charges.

"Let me get this straight," she said. "This perp . . ."

"Perp? Really?" Everett chuckled. "You watch too much TV."

"The police found this dude in his home after a domestic disturbance call. His wife is dead, and he's just watching TV in her bra and panties like nothing happened?" She read a little further. "And he claims he didn't even know she was dead in the next fucking room?"

"I know what you're thinking." Everett rolled his eyes and leaned back in his chair.

"It doesn't take a lawyer to realize this guy is guilty as fuck. How did someone else hear the murder taking place when he claims to have heard nothing while twenty feet away? This case is—"

"Unwinnable, Renee. I know."

"Maybe not. What's the evidence?"

"They list a knife, said bra and panties, and—" Everett lifted the paper and looked at it, his finger trailing along the lines of text in the document. *Eight-inch chef's knife*, he read to himself as he felt his heart rate rising.

"What's your problem?" Renee pursed her lips and shifted her weight before crossing her arms over her chest. "I was just trying to help."

"Shhh." Everett gestured with his hand before thumbing through the papers furiously. He pulled out a picture of the evidence bag with a knife in it. His eyes widened, and he tossed both papers down on the desk. "Do you know what this is?" Everett nearly danced in place at the discovery.

"What?" Renee leaned over and looked at the papers. "I don't see anything."

Everett pointed to the picture of the knife in a bag. "This is my golden case."

"What? How?" Renee tried to understand what he was saying.

His excitement was uncontrolled, and his words poured out of him like lava. "The evidence log lists an eight-inch chef's knife, right?" Everett picked up the log and showed it to Renee. "But what is this?" Everett lifted the evidence bag photo and put it in her face.

"I don't know, it's a small knife," she said with squinted eyes.

"Exactly! This is a five-inch serrated hunting knife! It means someone fucked up along the way, Renee. This could get the whole case tossed!" Everett was equal parts excited and full of guilt. He wanted his golden case so badly that he was willing to let a murderer go free. "If I can get this thrown out, the prosecution's office will most definitely take notice of me. Maybe not under the most ideal circum-stances, but they will know my name!" Everett looked around with wild eyes, as if the last few weeks of anguish and torment over this file had finally come to a turning point. "I have to tell Maria!" Everett hovered his hands around Renee's face, air kissing her on both sides. "Thank you!"

"I didn't do anything, but you're welcome?" Renee said as Everett shoved the files in the folder, grabbed his jacket, and hurried out of his office. "Bye, I guess?"

Everett jogged down the hall and clicked the elevator button. By the time he reached the ground floor, he was listening to the phone ring as he called his boss.

"Everett?" she said in a groggy voice. "It's ten o'clock. There better be a good reason for this." She yawned and

Everett cursed, not realizing how much time had passed pouring over the files.

"Only the best reason." He tried to catch his breath as he walked toward his car.

"Well, get on with it."

"I found my golden fucking case, pardon my français," Everett said with a smile that he was sure Maria could feel from her bedroom.

"What? Which one? This couldn't wait until morning?"

"I mean, I guess it could have, but I couldn't wait to tell you."

"Okay, enough with the suspense." Maria chuckled, her voice still heavy with sleep.

"The Ortiz case!"

"You—" Maria stammered. "What? How?"

"I found the fuck up, and it's a big one!"

"Okay, I'm listening now. You're right. This couldn't wait until morning."

"They messed up the evidence. The log lists an eight-inch chef's knife as the murder weapon, but a five-inch hunting knife is in the evidence bag. A fucking hunting knife. Do you know what that means, Maria? No prints, no murder weapon. Golden. Effing. Case." He cradled his phone against his shoulder and opened his car door.

"Well, shit. Bring the file to me first thing in the morning. Now go home and go to bed," Maria said with a sigh before the call ended.

CHAPTER EIGHTEEN

E verett whistled a tune as excitement shined through every airy step he took. The elevator dinged and opened, exposing the large fourth-floor office space. Everett smiled at the secretary.

"Good morning, Angelina."

"G-good morning," she stammered, caught off guard by the unusual friendliness.

Everett walked by Clarke's office. He stopped, took a few steps back, and poked his head in.

"It's a wonderful day, isn't it, Clarke?" Everett flashed a toothy smile.

"I don't know what has gotten into you, but you're being fucking annoying," Clarke said without looking away from his computer.

Everett didn't let Clarke's attitude shit on his parade. He took a few dancing steps toward Maria's office and stopped to straighten his jacket, tugging down the sleeves with a drawn-out exhale. Maria spotted him and waved him in.

"I'll call you back," Maria said as she tried to put the phone down. "Yes, I know. I'll call you right back." She slammed the phone down and smiled. "You seem to be in a better mood today."

Everett tossed the file on Maria's desk with a smile. Inside she would find a write-up detailing his discovery.

"Well, let's see what you've got here." Maria opened the folder and rubbed her chin as she looked through the notes, her eyes growing wider with each line. She flashed a smile and looked up at him. "I knew I had faith in you for a reason."

"At least one of us did," Everett said with a slight down-turn of his lips.

"I want a dismissal hearing, like, yesterday." Maria laughed. "I'll make the calls. The sooner this is dismissed, the sooner you can move to greener pastures. McNinch's office would have to be insane to reject your bid to switch sides after this. Now scoot so I can make these calls."

"What about the other cases on my desk? Someone has to help those people too," Everett said. He felt a little guilty for leaving work unfinished, but he had no interest in pursuing another defense case. He'd almost rather be unemployed.

"Clarke and I will handle them until we can find someone to take your spot."

"Tell her you want to go to dinner if you beat this case," Renee whispered in his ear.

He cleared his throat and tried not to jump. "Maybe if this turns out to be my golden case, we could go to dinner. You know, to . . . celebrate?"

Maria leaned back in her leather chair and smirked. "I think that's an excellent idea. How about Marcello's?"

"Oh, yeah! I've heard about that place. It's in that really swanky hotel down on—"

She pressed her teeth against her bottom lip and raised her eyebrows in a look Everett couldn't mistake for anything other than exactly what it was. "Win that case," she said, "and we can celebrate all night."

Everett nodded and headed for Clarke's office. He was glad to share the news with Maria, but his heart ached to tell Renee. In all their years of marriage, he'd never been able to rush home with a smile on his face to tell her he'd managed to get such a huge win. And he'd never have the chance to do it now. Sharing the news with her ghost wasn't the same.

He cocked his head when he rounded the corner and saw Clarke through the glass door, motionless at his desk and staring straight ahead. He tapped his knuckles against the door and opened it. "You okay?" He certainly didn't look okay. He'd never seen Clarke's smug face look so grim.

"I lost a huge case just now." He continued staring ahead, his eyes never meeting Everett's. "He told the police . . . everything."

"Could he have been coerced?"

"No, the dude fucking called the meeting himself." He picked up the report and cleared his throat. "I did it, I murdered the son of a bitch, and I don't feel bad at all. Fuck that guy. I ain't feel nothing but good about it." Clarke put the report down and looked up at Everett. "Those were his exact words before he detailed what happened and told police where to find the body. He didn't even wait for a fucking deal! That was our only card, and he laid it on the table for free."

For Clarke's sake, Everett tried to hold back his excitement about his own case. He wanted to share his news, but now didn't seem like the right time. Then again, Clarke never hesitated to crow about his successes, even when Everett was drowning in a manure pit of failures. "I finally got a break in the Ortiz case. Pretty sure we'll be able to get him released within the week."

"Well, shit. Who did you pay off to fuck up this colossally? You lucky son of a bitch." Clarke blew out a breath. "I'm happy for you, man. Truly," he said with a soft smile. "Did Maria suck your dick for this one?"

"No, can't say there has been any dick sucking in my morning. How about yours?" He waved his hand. "Nope, don't tell me."

"The only fucking I got this morning was from the long, hard dick of justice. I'm going to need some time to heal from this." He gave a light chuckle, but Everett thought he looked like he might cry.

"Use some lube next time," Everett said with a smirk.

"Yeah, I'll try to remember that if I'm ever bent over this desk again." He waved Everett off and went back to staring blankly into space.

Everett left Clarke's office and headed toward the bathroom. He pushed on the door, but it didn't open. A paper crinkled beneath his shoe, and he pulled it from the ground and looked at it. *Out of Order*.

"Are you kidding me?" Everett tapped his foot as his urge to pee grew stronger. *We're the only floor with clean bathrooms in this whole fucking building,* Everett thought with a groan as he clicked the elevator button.

Once the door opened, he tried to weigh out what floor might provide the least vomit-inducing experience. The first floor was the lobby bathroom, and every person who entered the building used it. He'd even seen the occasional homeless person sneaking in. Medical offices filled the second floor, and surprisingly, they were the worst of the choices. For being doctors, they didn't learn any bathroom hygiene in all those years of college. The last option was the third floor, filled to the brim with college-aged tech nerds, but there were more women than men on that floor, making it the safer option.

The elevator spread open on the third floor, and the thick

aroma of stale coffee wafted toward him. Everett was over-whelmed by the sounds of beeping, buzzing, and yelling into headsets. He shook his head as he walked past a hairy, greasy man seated at a table covered in computer monitors. With crumbs dangling within his unkempt beard, he wiped his chip fingers on his shirt before turning back to his computer. Everett looked around. There were only three women here now.

Oh, this isn't going to be good.

Everett hesitated for a moment before easing open the bathroom door. His mouth dropped in horror. *Fuck, I chose wrong,* he thought as the aching in his bladder intensified. The light illuminated yellow stains on the floor and walls, and yellow piss lines ran like a banner above the urinals. *How?* Everett eased back the door on the first of two stalls and froze at the sight before him. It was as if a shit bomb exploded and covered every surface in feces. He gagged and covered his nose, shaking his head. He'd take his chances with the urinals over the second stall.

"Wow, it's disgusting in here," Renee said. The aching in his pelvis drew him out of his trance just as Renee spoke. He jumped and almost peed himself, which probably would have been more hygienic.

"I'm so sorry. I can't wait." Everett ran to the least offen-sive urinal and unzipped his trousers.

His worst fears came true as a strange, middle-aged man came into the bathroom like a bull in a china shop. He charged in and nearly fell over. Renee stepped over a puddle of urine to stand closer to Everett, nearly hanging onto his arm. She grinned, her gaze looking down as Everett started to pee.

"Can you please not look?" His cheeks flushed red.

"I'm not fucking looking at you," the man said.

Renee laughed.

"I'm not talking to you," Everett grumbled.

The man's arm began moving far more than it should have, and it nearly touched Everett's elbow.

"Is that man—" Renee's mouth dropped open.

This cannot be happening. "This doesn't usually occur." Everett's face twisted, but he was trapped by his own unwavering stream.

"What?" The man looked into Everett's eyes, right through his soul.

"I wasn't talking to you, but god, how?" Everett shuddered as he zipped up his pants. "How can you even do that here? I'm a lawyer, and I'm fairly positive you're breaking several laws right now. Go to the stall or something!"

"I can't. There's shit in there." The man shrugged.

"Well, an alternative location could be your home, like a normal fucking person."

Everett zipped his fly and quickly washed his hands, spending an excessive amount of time using soap before turning on the dryer with his elbow. He held his hands out like a surgeon, clean and prepped, and contorted his body to open the bathroom door with any clothing-covered body part he could. The man released a low moan from his throat as Everett exited the bathroom. He cringed as the noise floated toward him and would forever live in his memory.

By the time Everett left the bathroom, sweat dripped from his forehead and down his sides. He would piss himself next time.

Renee hurried behind him as he stepped into the elevator.

"Why did you bring me here, anyway?"

"I didn't do it intentionally. I just thought about how I wanted to tell you—" Everett stopped as a man walked into the elevator and hit the button for the first floor.

"This elevator is going up," Everett said. He just wanted

to be alone. Well, as alone as he could be with his ghost wife beside him.

"Oh, is it? I guess I'm going for a ride." The man laughed at his own joke.

Everett's lips tightened. *I hate people.*

Renee was gone by the time the elevator doors opened on the fourth floor.

EVERETT THOUGHT of Renee as he ordered delivery from her favorite restaurant. He thought of her again as he set the table, complete with flowers in a vase he'd found under the kitchen sink. Lighting a candle, he thought of her again, but she didn't materialize. He plated her favorite dish—broccoli and chicken Alfredo—and set it in front of her chair. After sitting in front of his own plate with a sigh, he bowed his head, closed his eyes, and tried one more time to bring Renee to him.

I'm not with my family or in a public restroom or with a random horny woman. Please have dinner with me. He opened his eyes to an empty chair.

He lifted his fork with tears in his eyes and cut into his chicken fingers. Renee always teased him for ordering like a child, calling them his "chicken tendies." He'd give anything to hear her make that joke one more time. Even her ghost voice would do at this point. Tears slipped down his cheeks and splashed against the side of his plate. As he brought the first bite to his mouth, he heard a knock at the door.

It was a bit late for anyone to stop by. Still, he wiped his fingers on a napkin and went to the door, peering through the window before grabbing the knob. His stomach sank. Roman's sports car waited in his driveway. Everett glanced back at the kitchen table, panic sending off alarm bells through his mind. Roman already thought he'd lost his senses, and if he saw that Everett had set a table for two, he'd probably call the psych ward himself. He eased the door open just a crack.

"What do you need, Roman?" he said through the minimal opening.

"Jeez, that's no way to greet your brother. I just came by to make sure you were okay after you were being such a bitch at the barbecue. You haven't answered any of my calls."

Part of Everett had hoped his brother wanted to apologize, but that would have been too humble, and Roman Enders was anything but that.

"Not answering phone calls is called a hint," Everett said. "I'm in the middle of dinner, however, so we'll have to talk about what a bitch I am later." He tried to close the door, but Roman pushed his sausage fingers through the slit and forced his shoulder through the gap. Everett pushed against him, but he couldn't compete with someone who snorted creatine and considered weightlifting a fun pastime.

"Stop acting like this, Everett!" he shouted as he pushed into the house. Once he'd bullied his way in, he straightened his shirt and cracked his massive neck. His eyes landed on the table, and Everett's heart stopped functioning. "You got a hot date tonight?"

"Yes!" Everett said. His brother had given him the perfect out. "I'm expecting her any minute, so if you'll just—"

"Wait a minute." He walked to the table and stopped in front of Renee's plate. "Please tell me you aren't having a romantic dinner with your dead fucking wife."

Everett shook his head and scrambled for something to say, but his words got caught in a traffic jam between his brain and his tongue.

Roman held up his hand. "You don't even have to give

some bullshit lie. That's exactly what's going on because that's her favorite dish. You need help, bro. This is some next-level psycho shit. Like, right up there with Ted Brady, man."

"Get out!" Everett yelled, a spittle of rage flying from his mouth.

"You don't have to tell me twice, fucking whack job." Roman pushed past him and yanked the door open.

Everett stepped onto the front porch, his entire body shaking. "And it's Ted *Bundy*, you greasy moron!"

Roman slid into his car without a response and peeled out of the driveway, nearly taking out the neighbor's mailbox in the process.

"I thought you said you weren't with family," Renee said behind him.

Everett went back into the house and shut the door, avoiding walking through Renee as he stormed to the table. "Leave it to Roman to ruin a perfectly good day." He motioned for her to sit across from him.

Renee sat on the chair and gazed at the plate in front of her with a look of longing in her eyes. "Oh, Ev, you remembered."

He shoveled a chicken tender into his mouth and chewed. "Of course I did," he said to his plate. "Ralph's was our place, and that was your favorite."

His stomach clenched into a tight ball. There'd be no more dinners at Ralph's. No more kisses on his forehead in the evening when he crawled into bed. No more gazing into each other's eyes as they made love. But there hadn't been those things for a long time. He'd taken those moments for granted when they'd been at his fingertips, and now they rested at the bottom of the Mariana Trench. He'd never retrieve them.

His fork slipped from his hand and clattered against his

plate as a sob ripped through him. He didn't want to cry in front of Renee, but the grief was too much. Loving her was too much. "I can't keep living like this," he said from behind his hands. "I miss you, Renee. I miss you so goddamn much. I set up this dinner because Maria plans to push ahead with the dismissal as soon as possible, and I wanted to celebrate with you. A dinner with my wife's ghost. Maybe I am crazy." He pulled his hands away, expecting Renee to have disappeared as she always seemed to do when he got too emotional.

But she hadn't.

She reached her hand across the table, and though he knew they couldn't feel each other, his fingers went for hers. "I am so proud of you," she said. "Things will get better, I promise. Once you finally let me go, I'll be able to leave. But you have to let go, Everett."

Maybe this was the key all along and he'd been too stubborn to admit it. If he could win over Maria and let himself fall for her, his heart might begin to heal and Renee might be at peace. He'd have to try harder, and it started tomorrow.

CHAPTER NINETEEN

E verett spent his Sunday morning with his nerves rubbed raw over the dismissal hearing on Monday. Miguel's release would earn his place in a new firm, and that meant a dinner date with Maria. He rubbed a hand through his tousled brown hair and looked at himself in the mirror. He'd need to improve his appearance if he wanted to win her over, but there wasn't enough time to get rid of his gut. It was too bad men didn't have the advantage of makeup the way women did. The only thing he could really change to improve his appearance quickly was . . .

Everett snatched his keys from the coffee table and jogged to the car. Renee appeared in the passenger seat as he pulled out of the driveway.

"Put your seatbelt on," she said. "You don't want to end up like me."

"I will, Renee. I always put it on when I reach the stop sign by our house."

"What's the difference between there and the driveway?"

Everett shrugged and pulled the car to a stop at the sign

as he stretched the seatbelt across his stomach. "I don't know. Approximately two-hundred feet, I guess."

With a roll of her eyes and a shake of her head, she said, "Where are we going?"

"We're heading to town to see if Miranda has an opening. I want a new hairstyle." He turned onto a busy street and merged with a line of traffic. They continued on until the road split into a four-lane with rows of businesses on either side.

Renee pointed to the roller rink on the right side of the car. "Remember when we got booted out of there for getting too drunk?"

Everett laughed. "I nearly broke my arm in a fall. Who thought roller skating and alcohol were a good combination?"

"Apparently, we did." A light giggle slipped past her lips. "Oh, oh, remember that time at the movies?" Renee gestured toward the cinema as they drove past. "We got so drunk that we threw up blue and red ICEEs all over the floor."

"I remember! And I stayed to help the poor kid clean it up. What a mess. Why did we always get so sloppy?"

"I don't know. It's the only time you loosened up."

The smile fell from his face. "That's not true. I'm very loose."

Renee gave him a deadpan stare.

"Okay, I may have trouble relaxing sometimes . . ."

"*All* the time."

It hurt to admit it to himself, but he *was* a pretty boring man. Yet like a magician pulling silk scarves from a sleeve, Renee always managed to pull the boring out of him and insert a little fun into his life. The roller rink had been her idea for a date night. Then when he'd wanted to see a serious movie that would make them think, she'd insisted on a rom-com so they could get drunk and laugh. She'd been the Technicolor to his black-and-white ways.

"How could you stand to be with someone so stiff and boring when you were so lively and free?" Everett asked.

Renee shrugged. "Because you're handsome, you're a hard worker, and you could always make me laugh."

Everett let the corners of his mouth creep upward as he pulled into the salon's parking lot. He wasn't perfect, but Renee had loved him.

A neon sign that said Open spun in the window in front of them. He walked into the salon with Renee following behind him. He held the door open for her, forgetting that no one else could see her. When he realized his mistake, he let it go and cringed as it went through her back.

Everett sat in one of the stained lobby chairs and tried not to get a headache from the surge of fumes rushing toward him. The pungent aroma of burning hair, chemicals, and overpowering shampoos usually left him feeling unwell, but Renee always insisted he come here for a cut, and he wasn't ready to break that tradition just yet.

Renee rubbed a hand along the magazines and hair books with a forlorn look in her eyes. She probably missed getting her hair done. She'd disappear for hours and come back looking like a whole new woman after an afternoon at this very salon. Everett sighed. How many times had he overlooked the change in her appearance until she begrudgingly mentioned it? He should have told her more often how beautiful she looked. Just before she died, she'd had the tips of her dark hair bleached and dyed a deep plum. When the sun shone down on her, it exposed the silky purple hue and brought out the blush in her cheeks. He'd loved it, and he'd never taken the time to tell her.

Miranda caught sight of him and waved him over to her chair. "You in for a trim, honey?" she asked. Bright pink lipstick covered her lips, creating a sharp contrast against her tan skin. On anyone else it would have looked gaudy, but Miranda made it work.

"Yeah, I want to get a light trim and maybe try a new style," he said.

She nodded and wrapped a black smock around his neck as she plopped him into the chair. "Oh, Everett, I'm so sorry for your loss," Miranda said, a deep frown on her face. She looked at him in the mirror as she spoke and tugged a comb through his hair. "Renee had just been in here the week before, and she seemed *fine*. I had no idea she'd—"

"I know, me neither. I had no idea."

"What do you want done?" Miranda asked, changing the subject. Hair stylists always seemed to know when it was time to move to a new topic.

"Tips. Like, frosted ones." Everett brushed his hand through his hair as he talked. Miranda nodded as if she completely understood what he was asking for.

"No, please do not frost his tips," Renee interjected. "Everett, your hair is so nice and thick. Why don't you get the same style you do every time?"

Everett ignored her. "I want to take, like . . . twenty years off with this style." *I'll show Renee how "loose" I can get.* He pulled out his phone, did a quick search, and pointed to a picture of Justin Timberlake circa 1997.

"Oh, god, no," Renee whimpered helplessly from the corner as the hairdresser mixed the bleach and went to work.

"Have you dated since Renee passed?" Miranda asked.

"I've tried a little but—"

"No good?" She flashed a smile at him.

Everett shook his head. "Not even a little."

"We can go out for coffee or something, if it would make you feel better."

"Oh, that's very nice of you, but I think I'm realizing I'm not quite ready yet," Everett said with a genuine smile.

Renee's eyes went wide, and she blinked back her shock. "Miranda Billings, you are a married woman!"

Everett bit his tongue to hide his smile.

An hour of mundane conversation later, Miranda stared at Everett as if she were examining something strange and unfamiliar. Her lips were tight. Her eyes showed concern. Her nostrils flared with every breath. She spun Everett around and he saw himself in the mirror.

His mouth dropped open. "I look . . ." Everett patted his hair. "Oh god."

A fountain of laughter poured from Renee, entered his ears, and filled him with shame until his cheeks blazed red.

"I fucking told—" She choked on her laughter. "I told you not to frost your tips." She was nearly on the floor at that point, her cackles erupting in a painful sounding wheeze. "You look like . . . you've been doing meth every day . . . for six months!"

Everett stared at her with a frown as she righted herself and wiped her eyes.

"I mean, your body definitely isn't meth," she continued, "but your face with that hair? Definitely meth."

"I can fix it," Miranda said, sensing his dislike for his poor decision.

"You'll have to cut half my hair off!" he whined.

"No, not necessarily." She grabbed a sheet of hair samples and held it up to his head. "We could just color over it. Something close to what it was before. It may come out a little lighter than your natural color, but hey, it's not . . . this."

"Fine." Everett frowned as Miranda scurried away to mix up the color. He looked back to make sure she was gone. "I hate you, Renee."

"Me? What did I do? I told you not to."

"You made me feel like an uptight dolt."

"I'm sorry I made you feel that way, but I didn't mean you had to change the way you look, and I damn sure didn't mean to go do this." She pointed to his hair.

Miranda returned, interrupting Everett's conversation with the empty chair in the corner. "Okay, I'll have you fixed up in no time," she said with a strained voice as she started painting the color into his hair.

By the time Everett left the salon, he had the exact same haircut he always got and tips that were a shade lighter than his natural color. The blond undertones shimmered in the sunlight.

Damn it.

CHAPTER TWENTY

Everett kicked his feet up on the coffee table in his living room and shoved chicken poppers into his mouth with a smile. He turned to Clarke. "You should have seen McNinch's face in court last week." Everett mimicked the prosecutor's frowning face.

"That dude's gonna be your boss, you know." Clarke smirked as he grabbed a handful of chicken.

"I know, but I can still enjoy it for a moment, eh?" Everett sighed and dropped his head back. "Can I ask you a question?"

"Shoot," Clarke said with his mouth full.

"Am I uptight?"

"You?" Clarke laughed. "Oh yes."

"What?" Everett put his feet on the floor and sat up.

"You're a walking fidget spinner. Always doing things, never just relaxing. And if some minor inconvenience happens in your day, watch out, because the only train in Everett town is derailed." Clarke stopped chewing and looked at him. "I didn't mean it offensively, man."

"I know you didn't, but is this really how people see me?" *Is this how Renee saw me?*

"Sometimes." Renee appeared beside Everett, but he didn't look at her.

"I know what would help you relax." Clarke pulled a blunt from his pocket and twirled it around in his fingers.

"Clarke!" Everett's jaw dropped.

"I'm going to take a leap here and say you've never smoked weed in your life," Clarke asked as he lit one end and put the other in his mouth, sucking in the smoke.

"Don't let him smoke in here!" Renee sat up tall, eyes following the rising smoke.

"Maybe you shouldn't smoke in here." Everett stood and opened the sliding glass door, waving the smoke away as he walked back to the couch.

"Oh, it's fine. They did your pre-employment drug test already, right?" Clarke wiggled his eyebrows.

"Fine, give me the doobie." Everett waved his hand toward him.

"I will give you the blunt, because no one calls it a *doobie* anymore." Clarke handed it to Everett, who held it between his thumb and forefinger like it might explode.

"Everett, you do *not* have to do drugs to prove you can loosen up," Renee said with a sigh as she fanned the smoke away from her. Could spirits get a contact buzz?

Everett put the blunt to his lips and inhaled the hot smoke into his mouth. He coughed instantly and sent a puff of smoke into the air.

"The burn means it's working." Clarke laughed and took the blunt back. He inhaled and held it, shaking his head softly before blowing it out in a controlled exhale.

Everett hit it again, able to hold the smoke for a few seconds longer each time he took a turn. Renee sat back on the couch and twirled her hair.

"Why am I even here?" she whined.

"You could always leave," Everett said, his annoyance veiled by the giggly mood that washed over him.

"Me?" Clarke asked.

"No, not you. Sorry." Everett handed it back to Clarke and exhaled toward Renee. He relaxed and melted into the couch cushions. "Oh, I am *loose*." He drew out the word "loose" to ensure they all knew how relaxed he was.

"Men are idiots." Renee willed herself away.

"Hey!" Everett looked back at where Renee had been and frowned.

"What?" Clarke asked.

"Nothing, I swear I felt Renee here with me."

"You're just high." Clarke laughed and handed him the last bit of the roach.

"No, I'm not. I've seen Renee and even spoken to her," Everett said as he took the final hit.

"Yeah, okay." Clarke laughed and ate more chicken poppers. "You're very high."

"Maybe you're right," Everett said with a sigh as he sat back with his hands behind his head. Clarke got up and grabbed two beers from the fridge and handed one to Everett.

"Oh, poly-substance abuse. I'm wild." Everett took the bottle and twisted the cap, letting the bitter beer wash away the taste of smoke and weed.

"Even high, you're a fucking weirdo." Clarke shook his head and took a large sip of his beer.

"I'm not weird, just homeschooled." Everett laughed too hard at his joke.

"What does that have to do with anything?"

"I have weird social skills and anxiety about the dumbest shit. My childhood was a fucking free-for-all." Everett wiped his brow. "I'm not even sure what Renee saw in me." His high took a sudden dark turn.

"Probably your fat wallet."

Everett pulled out his wallet and opened it. "When I brush the cobwebs off, you'll see I do not have a fat wallet at all. Maybe it was my bedroom skills." He smirked.

Clarke scoffed. "I highly doubt that."

"What?" Everett stared at him.

"You seem like a 'let's keep our shirts on and turn the lights off' kind of lover."

"What? No!" Everett protested, even though Clarke was pretty much correct.

"How many women have you been with, Everett?"

"Two." His answer was quick and embarrassing. "Do I even want to ask you?"

"I'd say over twenty-five but less than fifty-five." Clarke laughed. "I have to say, from what I knew of your wife, she'd have needed an animal in bed."

Does a teddy bear count? Fuck. Everett groaned. *I really did push her away, didn't I?* "Maybe Maria will teach me her ways." Everett laughed and ended with an uncomfortable sigh.

"Dude, that woman is going to fuck *you*!" Clarke laughed.

"With any luck."

CHAPTER TWENTY-ONE

"**D**id you do something different with your hair?" Maria asked as she sat at the table.

"No, not really." Everett shrugged it off, making Maria squint her eyes.

She licked her finger and thumbed through the papers in front of her. "The hearing is with Judge Adams." She looked at her watch. "And we really have to get going if we want to make it there on time. It's not far, but lunchtime traffic is a bitch." She stood, grabbed her jacket, and hurried out of the office.

Everett grabbed his jacket off the back of the chair and followed her to her BMW in the parking garage. *Fancy.* Everett climbed into the roomy black SUV. *Is this what six-figures looks like?* He rolled down the tinted windows as Maria backed up and nearly hit the cars behind her. She seemed unfazed. *Renee also gave zero shits about nearly taking out every car around her,* he thought with a chuckle. He looked into the backseat to make sure Renee hadn't appeared, but it was empty.

"What's wrong?" Maria asked, cocking her head.

"Nothing. I was just admiring your backseat." Everett screamed internally at his social skills. Always grade C.

"Yeah, I can fit anything in my trunk as well."

Everett looked at her. *Which trunk does she mean? Oh god.*

She reached over and let her hand rest on his thigh. "You're nervous. Don't be. I'm right here with you." She smirked and her hand rubbed down his thigh and back up.

Everett put his arm over his lap, trying to hide his excitement from such a minute touch. "Thank you for coming." Everett smiled at her before he looked out the window, trying to distract himself from the brewing excitement. He watched the shops whiz by. "How fast are we going? The speed limit is thirty."

"I'm pretty much going thirty-ish."

He looked over and saw the speedometer wiggling away at fifty. "What if we get pulled over? That will ruin my hearing."

"Relax, Everett. I'll just tell the officer that I'm a lawyer and they'll let me go."

Everett looked at her with wide eyes. "Does that really work?"

"If you undo a few buttons before they get to your window, it does," she said with a giggle.

Everett looked down at his chest. "Unfortunately, I don't think I have the same credentials."

Maria pulled up to the large brick building in the heart of the city. She smoothed her skirt as she got out of the car, and Everett tugged down his sleeves, crisping the fold.

"Let's go blow this case wide open," Everett said as he walked toward the door with proud, methodical steps. He imagined theme music playing around him. Crack shot lawyer theme music. The music stopped as he tried to finagle the door open with his sleeve and half slammed himself into it. He cleared his throat, pulled it open, and let Maria go past him.

"Real smooth," she said with a wink.

Everett and Maria walked down a large hallway toward wooden doors lined with gold trim. Fancy tropical plants crawled upward and spread like fans on either side. The plaque on the wall highlighted Judge Adams' name. They both took a deep breath before opening the double doors.

Heavy air circulated through the courtroom, as if the anxious exhalations of previous murderers still hovered in the room. Maria's heels tapped against the tiled floors as she walked to the table for the defense.

"Ms. Armani, it's been a while since I've seen you in my court," Judge Adams said, smiling from beneath his round-rimmed glasses. "And Mr. Enders, this is not the first, nor the last, I presume?"

Everett tried to mimic Maria's confidence. "No sir," he said as he sat in the wooden chair. There was a loud scraping noise when he tried to scoot closer to the desk. *Sorry*, he mouthed to the judge. His gaze landed on McNinch, whose usually handsome face looked more like he'd been sucking on something sour. Everett's leg shook under the table, and Maria reached over and steadied it with a soft touch.

"Stop, you're making *me* nervous," she said before crossing her legs. She opened the file and shuffled her paperwork. "This is just a formality. It's as good as done, so there's nothing to be worried about."

"Sorry," he whispered.

The judge called the court to order and motioned to Everett.

Everett got to his feet and cleared his throat. "I am requesting a motion to dismiss this case due to improper handling of evidence. The knife listed in the log is an eight-inch chef's knife, but in the evidence photo, the knife is an approximately five-inch serrated hunting knife. Clearly, this knife is not the knife that committed this murder, neither by the log nor the injuries sustained by the victim. Without the fingerprints or a murder weapon, there is no other recourse but to dismiss this case."

The judge licked his lips before motioning to McNinch. The prosecutor stood, cleared his throat, and adjusted the jacket of his pleated navy-blue suit that accentuated the blue of his eyes. Everett suddenly felt insecure about his plain black warehouse suit that was too baggy in the shoulders.

"The prosecution doesn't have much to say, unfortunately. A huge mistake was made in the chain of custody for the weapon in question."

Colossal mistake, actually, Everett thought.

"Do you have any other evidence against the client that would allow this trial to move forward?" the judge asked.

"Nothing that isn't circumstantial, Your Honor." McNinch dropped his gaze. Despite the situation, his shoulders remained upright and confident as he glanced sideways at Everett.

"Then I have no choice but to dismiss this case without prejudice," the judge said. From the way he hesitated, it seemed as if he felt the defendant was guilty.

"Thank you, Your Honor," the lawyers responded in unison as they gathered their paperwork.

His brain buzzed, preventing him from speaking or even hearing what anyone said next. After shaking the judge's hand, he pivoted on mechanical legs and walked back toward a grinning Maria. Before he made it to the table, he felt a hand on his shoulder. He turned and found himself face to face with McNinch.

"Well played, Mr. Enders. I've heard you were meticulous with details, and I have to admit I worried you'd find a mistake I missed. I just didn't think it would be one that would turn the whole case on its head. We could use a set of eyes like yours, if you ever care to join the light side." McNinch looked at Maria. "No offense."

"None taken," Maria said. "He's been wanting to switch teams for a while now. As much as I'll miss his annoying attention to detail, who am I to hold him back?" Maria brushed her hair behind her ears and flashed a flirty smile at Everett before grabbing his arm and leading him toward the doors. "I'll be in touch soon," she called back as they walked away.

Everett and Maria made their way back to her BMW. Inside the SUV, she turned to face him, her hand sliding onto his thigh again. "So that just leaves one loose end. When's our celebratory dinner?"

His tongue turned to a wad of cotton in his mouth. *Tonight*, he wanted to shout, but that would sound too eager. He had to hide his desperation and excitement and play this cool. "How does this weekend sound?"

"Sounds like a date," she said with a bite of her lip. "I'll call McNinch and set up your transfer, but if our weekend goes well, you'll have to handle the disclosure conversation." She winked and got out of the car.

EVERETT STOOD in the kitchen with a bottle of vodka. He twisted off the cap and poured some of the clear liquid into a glass. The harsh aroma of cheap liquor filled his nose as he brushed his hair back. Maria had sent him home for the day and told him he could take the rest of the week off while she worked out the details of his big move.

Renee appeared in front of him with her eyebrows lifted in judgment.

"What?" he asked with a minute shake of his head.

"Okay, we need to talk about your attitude toward life. Ever since your evening with Clarke, you're . . ." She stopped, trying to choose her words carefully. "Not yourself. Also, you're drinking at ten in the morning."

"I just realized how much of my life I've missed out on." He took a gulp of liquor and plopped onto the couch. "I couldn't please you. People think I'm boring. And frosted tips make me look like I went on a six-month meth bender while still managing to eat." He patted his belly.

"You pleased me fine," Renee interjected, her lips drawn tight. "I just wish you were half as hungry for me as you were for that damn girl on the couch."

Everett knew he didn't please her enough. Renee used to be a wild woman. Much too wild for him. She always asked for things he couldn't bring himself to do. Slap her, choke her, or fuck her like he wasn't who he was—a boring square. She deserved to be with a man who could fuck her until she didn't know her own name. She wanted to be fucked stupid.

Guilt washed over him for acting so reckless and starved with the woman from the dating app. Renee would have *loved* it if he'd touched her like that. Like he'd touched her in the beginning. Their first few months together were a blaze of sexcapades. He couldn't keep his hands off her, but he'd been such a reserved lover, oftentimes requesting to keep the lights off or leave his shirt on because he was so insecure about his body. It all spiraled downward from there.

"If I could do it all over again, I would rip the clothes off your body and devour every inch of you," he said with a growl. The alcohol had loosened him up and quieted his mind, allowing his dick to scream louder.

"What if we touched ourselves?" Renee flirted back, her full lips loose and pouty.

Everett kept his eyes on her as she moved to the chair across from him. She hiked the hem of her slip and let her hand wander between her legs. A soft moan eased past her lips, and her other hand lowered the strap on her slip, revealing her soft breast. Everett lifted his eyebrows and hurried to unbutton his pants and expose himself to her in ways he never had when she was alive.

"Tell me more," she whispered as she spread her legs further.

"I would lay you down and fuck you better than I've ever fucked you. Harder than I've ever fucked you," Everett said with low and sultry words. His tone was gravelly and intermingled with pleasure as he watched her rub herself. He did the same. Her eyes locked on his dick as he stroked himself.

He longed to put his hands on her and inside her. His motions quickened as he watched her back arch with pleasure, and his breath grew ragged as his motions became jerky. He dropped his head back as he came.

"Fuck," Everett groaned. "How am I supposed to move on if you can please me like that?"

Renee smiled with pride while lowering her slip. Everett reached for some tissues and wiped his hands.

"It's true, you guys don't masturbate the same way in front of us." She laughed, and Everett's cheeks flushed with embarrassment.

"Jesus Christ," Everett shook his head. "We were having such a good moment."

CHAPTER TWENTY-TWO

E verett willed Renee into the middle of their bedroom. A mound of clothing covered the bed and nearly reached the top of his head when he stood up. Jewelry, makeup, and hair products littered the floor, making the room look as if a cosmetology tornado had blown through.

"What are you doing?" Renee looked around with wide eyes. "Why are my things scattered everywhere?"

"I have my date with Maria tonight. What if I want to bring her back to the house? To the bedroom? It looks like I'm still married," Everett said as he pulled a trash bag off the roll and shook it open.

"Please don't put my stuff in trash bags." She looked around at all the stuff she'd enjoyed when she was alive.

"Where do you suggest I put them?"

"I don't know!" she squealed. She sat on the only corner of the bed that wasn't covered by the remnants of her life. "Oh, the blue dress." She smiled as Everett held it up. "I wore that on our first date, remember?"

"Yeah, you brought us to the saddest zoo in all of animal husbandry history."

"I didn't know!"

"And then we spent the rest of the evening drinking two-dollar Long Islands and getting drunk at Applebee's. Pretty low point in our lives, I'd say." Everett smirked.

"Good times. Why were we such alcoholics?" She pointed to a short black skirt. "Remember when I dragged you to the club and you spent the whole time worrying about all the code violations you witnessed? Date a lawyer, they said. It'll be fun, they said." She rolled her eyes.

"Yeah, I remember. That rando girl grinded on me before doing a line of coke off my hand. Unhygienic." He shuddered at the memory. "Before I realized what she was doing, she was already nose to palm." Everett picked up a bikini and wiggled his eyebrows. "Remember these?"

"Remind me," she said with a sultry smile.

"We were having sex behind a dune in St. Augustine, and the police officer found us. We acted like we didn't speak English. He got so flustered he let us go! I'm still not entirely sure what Spanish words I said. It's like I was just vomiting verbs."

Renee started laughing at the memory. "I was very surprised you took the lead on that one. I was just going to push my tits up and beg for forgiveness."

"You can't use your tits for everything, Renee," Everett said.

"I got my job at the club, I got out of several speeding tickets, and I got you with them."

"You have great tits, but they weren't my favorite part of you."

"What part was your favorite?" she pried.

"Your ass. How you always had to go up a size in jeans because of it." He made a low noise from deep within his throat. He picked up her jeans and smiled as he tossed them in the bag.

"What are you doing with them?" Renee asked.

"Donating them."

"Well . . . can you keep some of them? My favorites?" Her eyelashes fluttered.

"Why? It's not like you can wear them now. And besides, we're supposed to figure out how to get you to cross over, not keep you here, attached to expensive designer fabrics."

"Whatever." Renee crossed her arms.

Everett turned his attention to her makeup.

Renee looked at him with an aggressive stare. "No, not my makeup!" Renee screamed as Everett dragged all the items off the dresser and into the garbage bag. "This is killing me, physically hurting me, Everett. Do you know how much money that cost? That one tube of mascara in your hand was forty-five dollars."

He twirled the black tube with his mouth agape. "Forty-five dollars for this?" He picked up the others. "How many fucking overpriced tubes of lies do you have here?"

"Lies?"

"No one's eyelashes are that long, nor are they meant to be. I liked your eyelashes the way they were." Everett picked up a pallet of eyeshadow, and Renee nearly fell to her knees as he tossed it in with its fallen comrades.

Renee closed her eyes and clutched her stomach with one hand. "God, this is painful."

"You always wanted to look like someone else. If I could have done this when you were alive, I would have. I loved your face as it was. Especially first thing in the morning before you scurried off to the bathroom to hide it."

"I didn't hide it, I enhanced it," she said. "I can't watch any more of this." Renee disappeared and left Everett alone to clean up the mess she left him with. In more ways than one.

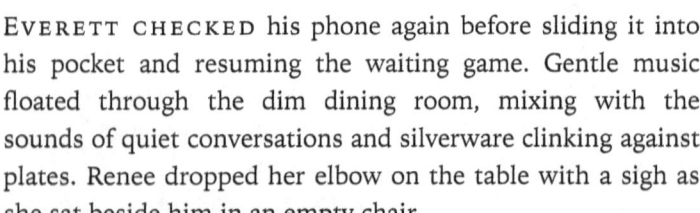

EVERETT CHECKED his phone again before sliding it into his pocket and resuming the waiting game. Gentle music floated through the dim dining room, mixing with the sounds of quiet conversations and silverware clinking against plates. Renee dropped her elbow on the table with a sigh as she sat beside him in an empty chair.

"I think you're getting stood up, dude." Renee folded her arms and looked around. "She's thirty minutes late."

"Thirty minutes doesn't mean much to lawyers, Renee. We can lose that time just trying to exit the damn office. Everyone always needs something."

The waiter approached, wearing a confused look and carrying a pitcher of water. He filled Everett's glass without asking who he was having such an in-depth conversation with. His task finished, he hurried away.

"God, I really need to stop talking to you in public," he whispered.

"If tonight goes well, maybe this won't be a problem anymore."

Maria appeared at the far end of the room. A black cocktail dress traced her outline, stopping halfway up her thighs, and strappy black heels drew his eyes to her toned legs. He'd never seen her in anything other than business attire. His mouth went dry as he lifted his hand and caught her attention. She rushed toward him, clutching a small black purse against her side.

"I'm so sorry! Clarke—"

"Say no more," Everett said with an understanding chuckle. Clarke was a pain in everyone's ass.

"I know, but I was really looking forward to this, and now

I'm all flustered." Maria fanned herself as she draped the silver chain of her purse over the back of the chair.

"You're fine." Everett picked up the menu.

"Give her a compliment, you dunce." Renee shook her head.

Everett cleared his throat. "You look really nice today. Not that you don't look good every day, but I just wanted to make sure—"

"I know what you mean, Everett. Stop being so nervous. It's just me. Just pretend I'm sitting next to you in court."

"Somehow, that's worse," he said.

The waiter stopped at his table and looked at Maria with a raised eyebrow, as if he didn't expect a real person to show up tonight. He offered her water and she nodded.

"Wine too, please," she said.

The waiter returned with the pitcher and a cold bottle of wine. He filled her water before holding the wine in the palm of his hand, showing off the label.

"Our finest." He smiled.

"Oh, we don't need the—"

"Yes you do, shut up," Renee snapped.

Everett stopped speaking and just smiled and nodded. The waiter scrunched his face before filling the glasses.

"God, I don't remember you being this bad on our dates," Renee said. "But maybe it's been a long time since we had an actual date." She licked her lips as she leaned over and looked at the menu. "Is there anything heart healthy here? With all the junk you've eaten this week, you can't afford another cheat day."

"I've never been here before. Anything look good on the menu?" he asked Maria with an uncomfortable smile on his face.

"I was thinking something fattening and messy. Alfredo maybe?"

"Oh, that does sound good," Everett responded.

Renee slammed her hands on the table, but they passed through the white tablecloth, ruining the effect. "I fucking give up!"

The waiter approached with his notepad, and they both ordered the Alfredo with penne pasta. Maria added chicken, but Everett was turned off by the additional cost. *Four dollars for a handful of chicken? No thanks.*

"No, yeah, don't add the only part of that meal that would be healthy-ish for you." Renee rolled her eyes and sat back. Everett really wished he could will Renee away. She was making everything worse.

The waiter left and they fell into an awkward silence.

Renee threw her hands up in exasperation. "Say something, you fool. You never shut up any other time."

"How has it been at the office?" he finally asked.

"Awful. Clarke has become intolerable without you. He's always in my office now, bugging me about anything and everything." She laughed and took a sip of wine. Her lipstick left a crimson smudge on the glass.

"He's just harmless entertainment."

Maria shrugged. "I think he hopes I'll hand him a case like yours."

"Did you hand me that case on purpose?" Everett lifted his eyebrows.

"Not entirely. I had heard some whispers that the case against Miguel was shaky at best, but I looked that file up and down and couldn't find the flaw. I knew there was *something* there, I just didn't know what or how big."

"Who's the bug in your ear?"

"Believe it or not, it's your soon-to-be boss. McNinch doesn't even realize when he's said too much. Completely oblivious. Sometimes the dude just hands me a case on a silver platter."

Everett battled with himself over the question he wanted to ask. *Fuck it.* "Did you and McNinch ever date?"

Renee shot a harsh glare at him. "First you waste time talking about work, now you're digging into her sex life? I'd better start making myself at home in that white fucking room. I'll probably never leave."

Maria was unflappable. "I knew him back in law school. We had a few dates and spent some nights together." Maria took another sip of wine. "We've never done anything since becoming rivals. Sometimes he forgets that's what we are, though. He's not really my type."

The waiter came and placed their plates of food on the table. Maria dived into hers as if she hadn't eaten all day, but Everett ate much slower, enjoying every bite and trying to avoid staining his dress shirt.

"No lunch again?" he asked. Maria shook her head and smiled. "Been there too many times myself." He smiled back before putting a forkful of pasta into his mouth.

"You guys are eating like pigs at the trough." Renee scrunched her nose.

Everett's fork slipped from his hand and sent a smear of sauce down the front of his shirt. He wanted to crawl under the table and never emerge. He lifted it from his lap and placed it beside his plate. "I feel like I'm screwing this date up." With a frown, he looked down at the table.

"You aren't. I know how you are when you're nervous and when you're not." Her smile was so strong it shined in her eyes. It was a genuine smile without pity or condescension.

Everett returned the smile but with much less confidence.

"Is this the first date you've had since your wife passed?" Maria asked.

Renee perked up at the question.

"No," Everett said as the memories of his awkward dates flooded back to him. The first literally ran from him, and the second one saw him as nothing more than a throbbing piece of meat. "But the other two were terrible."

"At least your third is a smashing success," Maria said. "I've had a wonderful time so far."

"Yeah, if you don't count dribbling food down my shirt." He looked at the stain and a fresh shock of embarrassment buzzed through him.

"Well, I was late. The two things cancel each other out, making it a great date."

The waiter brought the check, and Maria reached for it.

"No way, I got it." Everett grabbed the little black book and looked at the damage.

"Don't you dare react, Everett," Renee said. "It's fine. The cost is fine. Watch your face. You are *terrible* with your face."

Everett forced a smile onto his face as he processed the one-hundred-dollar price tag. *Finest fucking wine. I could buy three bottles of unfine wine for this cost and not be able to tell the difference.* He opened his wallet, withdrew his credit card, and placed it in the book.

"That was fantastic, definitely worth the money," he lied.

They walked to the hotel lobby together, hesitation hindering every step like a rope around their ankles. She'd hinted at getting a hotel room when they first talked about this restaurant, but Everett wasn't so sure he could go through with it. Scrubbing Renee from his bedroom had been a waste of time as well. He didn't want to rush into bed with Maria the way he'd nearly gone balls deep with Megan. It wasn't just sex with her. He *liked* her. But what if sex was all she wanted?

They stopped at the glass doors, and Everett turned to Maria with a pained smile. "I don't know what you expected from tonight, but I don't think I'm ready just yet. If that spoils the date, maybe you can do something to make us even again, because I'd really like to see more of you."

"What the fuck are you doing?" Renee shrieked. "Take it back! Tell her never mind, you'd love to take her upstairs and make love to her."

"I completely understand," Maria said. She moved closer and placed a kiss on his cheek. "You haven't ruined anything. You just need more time, and that's okay."

Everett helped her into a cab and ran his hand through his hair as it pulled away from the curb. "There's maybe a fifty-fifty chance she'll call me back."

"Looks like you didn't need to throw all my shit out after all." Renee shook her head.

CHAPTER TWENTY-THREE

E verett walked into the high-rise building downtown, not too far from his old job. The sun glared down at him and reflected off the glass. He shielded his eyes and smiled before heading into the building. His finger moved along the directory until he found his office. After taking the stairs to the second floor, he walked down a hallway that seemed to go on forever, with offices dotting each side until he reached room 202. He opened the door with his new key and breathed in the scent of the freshly cleaned office space. It smelled like lemon and chemicals. He set down a box of belongings and glanced around the room. The space was pretty drab compared to his old office.

At least this place has an opaque door and real walls.

He took a mental note of where he would hang pictures and his credentials. A lanky little plant sat on the desk by his computer. Its leaves reached toward the sky, trying to find light. He grabbed the plant and stuck it on the ledge in front of the little window overlooking the bustling city street. Below him, the sidewalk paved the way for businesspeople wearing suits and gripping briefcases. There were no clubs or idle distractions here. A food truck stood at the corner, and Everett made a mental note to test it out on his lunch break.

He jumped at the sound of a knock on the door and adjusted his collar as he sat in the padded computer chair. "Come in!" Everett called out.

The door opened and McNinch walked into his office. "Good morning, Everett. I hope you're finding things to your liking." McNinch took a seat in one of the chairs across from Everett's desk and crossed his legs.

"No, yeah, everything is really nice. I actually have walls, so that's good."

"You didn't have walls in your last office?" he asked with a laugh.

"The whole office was surrounded by glass. Privacy was in short supply."

"Oh yeah, no, not here. Shit, you could nap in here and I wouldn't notice."

"I won't be napping, but good to know." Everett smirked.

McNinch pulled two files from under his arm and slid them across the oak desk. Everett touched the tan manilla folders. While they felt no different from those at his last job, they were different in ways that made his heart thrum with excitement. He opened the first one.

"Rape of a victim less than fourteen." Everett frowned as he opened the other folder. "Attempted murder with gross bodily harm." Everett pursed his lips. "I'm so excited to prosecute these guys instead of helping them catch a break they don't deserve."

"These cases are rough, but there are some holes in both of them. I need you to find the holes and plug them. You have intimate knowledge of the inner workings of your old office. Help us put these people where they belong."

Everett nodded and closed the files. "Who's defending these two?"

"Clarke, of all people," McNinch said. He spoke Clarke's name the way most people did—with a hint of distaste. Even then, Everett felt a pang of longing for his friend and a bit of guilt for going against him in the ring.

"He always thought he was a better lawyer than me. Game on." Everett cocked a grin.

"You can out-lawyer Clarke any day." McNinch nodded and stood before smoothing his dark gray suit pants and looking down at Everett. He cleared his throat. "It's a little awkward to bring this up on your first day, but I heard you went on a date with Maria."

"Is that going to be a problem?" Everett's chest tightened. Despite his fears that she wouldn't call him again after he didn't jump into bed with her, she'd spoken with him every day since. They even had plans that evening. If McNinch didn't give the okay, he'd be cooking dinner for one instead of two.

McNinch tightened his lips. "No, it's not a problem, but I expect utmost discretion regarding our cases. I promise to never pit you two against each other because that would be highly unethical, but don't give her any information she can use against us."

Like you've given to her so many times before? "Understood." Everett nodded and faked a smile.

"Good. Now get started on those cases. And remember . . . keep your business shit and your personal shit separate or you'll find yourself without a job."

Everett nodded again and gulped back his anxiety as McNinch left his office.

EVERETT FOLDED the collar of his maroon polo shirt and smoothed the wrinkles with his hands. His jeans hugged his waist like an iron fist. He'd forgotten to buy a size up when he'd gone up a size. He brushed gel through his hair with his fingers and washed his hands when he was satisfied with the style.

"You may be fat, but you're handsome," he whispered, trying to encourage himself.

The doorbell rang, and Everett tried not to run all the way to the door. Renee had given him a pep talk as he got ready, and she specifically said he shouldn't seem too eager. She'd disappeared once she'd helped him pick an outfit, promising to leave the two of them alone for the evening as long as he tried to let things progress with Maria.

As he opened the door, Renee's advice about playing it cool evaporated from his mind. "Wow, you look . . . stunning." Everett didn't mean to sound so enamored, but he couldn't help himself as his eyes scanned her body.

She'd curled her hair, and the sultry scent of her perfume engulfed him in a warm embrace. Her cleavage peeked from the top of her deep-purple tank top. The longer he stared, the more her cheeks flushed.

"Are you going to invite me in?"

Right. Everett laughed uncomfortably and stepped aside to let her in. Her hips swayed as she walked, and Everett found himself staring at her ass in her tight black leggings. He closed the door behind her and took a deep breath.

"Sorry, I'm not good at this," he said.

"I wish you'd stop apologizing as if you have any intention of changing who you are." Maria's lips tightened into a thin line, and Everett frowned. Maria elbowed him and laughed. "I like who you are, awkwardness and all."

The alarm on the stove saved him from having to reply, and he rushed to the kitchen. He pulled the pan of chicken parmesan out of the oven and placed it on the counter. Renee had helped him cook, and while it hadn't been easy to follow her instructions, it smelled as if she'd made it herself.

Everett brought Maria a plate of chicken parm nestled on a pile of pasta and covered in a rich, creamy spaghetti sauce. He placed it in front of her, and her eyes followed it.

"Wow, Everett, this looks and smells incredible."

"It's Renee's recipe." Everett closed his eyes. *Idiot.* He looked around for Renee, expecting her to appear at the sound of her name, but she didn't. *Thank god.*

"Are you okay? You look nervous," she asked as she twisted the spaghetti around her fork.

"Yeah, I'm fine." Everett let the tempting scent of his dinner draw his attention back to the plate. His sweaty hand fumbled over the fork as he drew another bite of food to his mouth. A soft groan formed in his throat and slipped past his lips. "I think I outdid myself."

"This is orgasmic," Maria agreed. A little sauce slipped past her lips and painted her chin. Instead of making a fuss, she laughed and wiped it away with a napkin.

"Do you want some wine?" Everett asked, knowing he bought her the best wine he could find on sale at the store.

"Do you have any beer?"

He smiled at her simplistic tastes as he rose from the table and fetched a can from the fridge. Never in a million years had he pegged Maria as a beer drinker. The surprising facts he learned each time they were together kept adding up to someone he was beginning to like very much.

She took a hearty swig and continued eating. "Is it okay if I ask a tough question?" she said through a mouthful of noodles and sauce.

"I wouldn't expect anything less from an attorney," he said with a laugh.

"Do you think you're ready to date so soon after losing

your wife? I like you, Everett, but I don't have time for games. I don't even have time in general."

Everett thought as he drew another forkful toward his mouth. The question wasn't as difficult as Maria imagined, and the answer came naturally. "You're the first person who I felt like I *could* date since losing Renee."

"That doesn't necessarily answer the question." Her lips tightened as she placed her fork on her plate.

"I can't guarantee it won't be a struggle sometimes, but I'm willing to try if you are. I don't have time for games or bullshit either. Losing Renee taught me to stop taking things for granted, and that includes how I spend my time." He shook his head. "But I'm not the only one in this equation. I don't even know if I can give you what *you* need."

"How so?"

"I imagine you being into someone like Clarke or McNinch—cocky and confident. Suave in all the right settings. Then there's me . . ."

Maria crossed her legs and dropped her chin into her hand as her elbow rested on the table. "There's nothing inherently wrong with not being 'suave' or 'cocky.' Those traits aren't attractive to me. Also, I would rather put my arm in a wood chipper than go out with Clarke, just so we're clear." She smiled. "You make me *laugh*. I can't tell you how many times I went back into my office while thinking how lucky Renee was. I *want* to laugh and be happy at this point in my life. I'm sick of being serious and having to toe the line. I want to be with someone who can help me relax a little."

Everett's heart swelled at her words, though he struggled to find the truth in them. Renee never thought he could loosen up and enjoy life. Maybe he just couldn't enjoy the life she wanted to live.

Everett placed the plates in the sink and walked to the

couch with another set of beers. He set them on the table as Maria sank into the couch and got comfortable. He sat beside her, and she draped her legs over his lap. The warm heat of her skin sent a shiver through him.

"We gonna Netflix and chill? Emphasis on the chill," Maria said with a yawn.

"That's not what that means," he said, remembering learning the definition firsthand not that long ago.

"Screw innuendos. I'd tell you if I wanted to Netflix and fuck."

Everett kept his hands at his sides until he finally gained some courage and rubbed her leg with one of them. She groaned and Everett stared at her soft, full lips as they spread slightly to allow the sound to roll off her tongue. Excitement grew in his lap, and he hoped she couldn't feel it.

"Is that what I think it is?" she said coyly.

Shit. "Maybe," Everett whispered and looked back at the TV.

Maria sat up and rubbed him through the front of his jeans. "It's what I thought it was."

Everett shivered at the touch, so confident and aggressive. She leaned into him, her mouth closing in on his. When their lips met, he accepted her affection readily. Maria climbed onto his lap, and his hands went to her hips, his fingers racing along her curves. She moved against him, grinding her warmth over his length. Every cell in his body craved her.

So why did it feel so wrong?

"Maria." He pulled away.

She looked down at him as if she'd never been rejected a day in her life. Her expression wasn't angry, but the frustration was clear. She took a deep breath and climbed off of him, falling onto the couch with a sigh. "Too soon?"

"Maybe a little. I just . . ." He tried to think of the best way to say what he felt without sounding like a whining child. "I just don't want to mess this up. I want you, believe me, I want you. I've left your office hard more times than I can count. I've thought about you during our late nights at work, when the office was dark and we were the only two in the building."

The frustration on her face washed away, and a genuine smile replaced it. "Oh, you have no idea how many times you've fucked me in my office." She laughed as she brushed her hair behind her ear. "I'm not in a rush, Everett. I want to see where this goes. Just don't leave me waiting too long." Her hand grazed his thigh as she smoothed her shirt over her hips. "Maybe we can spend some time together at the conference."

Everett brushed his hand through his hair. "Yeah, McNinch mentioned something about that. I don't think I'm gonna go."

"You have to go," Maria said.

Everett groaned. "He said this business trip is optional, and I really don't want to go."

"This is the biggest conference for attorneys in the US. The best way to get your name out there is to go." She sat up taller, her stare boring into him.

Everett knew she was right. The most impressive and high-profile lawyers attended this event in Vegas each year. The skills you learned and the techniques you could acquire from the guest speakers were invaluable. And it was all expenses paid.

When she didn't stand down, Everett caved. "Fine. I'll tell McNinch I'm in."

"Good." Maria patted his thigh and opened her mouth in a yawn. "I'm going to get going."

"You aren't mad at me, are you?" he asked as he stood and walked her to the door.

"For not having sex with me? No. What kind of woman

do you think I am?" She leaned closer and kissed him with a gentleness he didn't expect from her. Her lipstick rubbed off on his lips and her scent lingered on his skin.

He watched her leave with a hollowness in his heart, a hole Renee left behind. Maria wanted to fill that empty space —and he wanted to fill her—so why couldn't he let her get closer? It wasn't only about sleeping with someone else after Renee. He worried he'd screw it up because he was starting to have real feelings for Maria. Renee made him feel guilty about being a poor lover and a boring human being. She didn't use those exact words, but the sentiment was there. How could he be a boring lover to someone as sexy and confident as Maria? He might ruin things if he fucked her, but he might ruin things if he *didn't* fuck her.

Well, Fuck.

CHAPTER TWENTY-FOUR

The airport was a traumatizing place for Everett. There were so many people coughing, sneezing, and touching every surface. Even with Maria in tow, sweat gathered and dripped down his sides. Rows of people snaked through the screening area. Everett and Maria were already running late for their flight, and this would only cut things that much closer.

Everett shifted his weight uncomfortably as people jammed in front of him, behind him, and even somehow on the sides of him. A man beside him released a hacking cough, and Everett's jaw clenched. Beads of sweat raced down his back.

"Have you ever been to Vegas?" Maria asked.

"Sin City? No."

"I went five years ago with my ex-husband. He nearly lost our house there."

Ex-husband? His stomach sank, and not just from holding his pee since he'd arrived. He cleared his throat. "I didn't realize you were married before."

"You didn't? I thought everyone knew. He's the face on my

dartboard at the office. He cheated on me and ran off to the Cayman Islands with some hot eighteen-year-old he met at his job . . . as a teacher."

"Oof." Everett shivered.

"Next," called a gruff voice from behind the conveyor belt. Everett walked toward the man and waited for directions.

"Shoes, bags, and anything in your pockets, including phones, in the bucket," the man said in a monotonous tone.

"Quick question . . ." Everett looked around at the stacked trays at the end of the conveyor belt. "Do you guys sanitize these after each use?"

"Yeah, sure," the man said, dismissing him with a wave. The answer was clearly a lie.

Everett took a deep breath as he slipped his shoes off and put them in a bin that may have contained a thousand other shoes today alone. He tried not to picture the amount of foot fungus spores clinging to the plastic before placing his phone into the box along with his keys. The guard motioned Maria through the metal detector. She stepped through, pausing as they scanned her body. Everett followed with a cautious step as the realization dawned on him that tons of other dirty feet had walked on that very floor. The alarm sounded around him before he could reach the other side.

"Do you have any other metal on you?" an equally gruff woman asked him. She looked as if she survived on donuts and Marlboro Reds.

"I don't think so," Everett said as he checked his pockets.

"Keys? Belts? Jewelry?"

Everett remembered his belt and worked it off, tossing it into the filthy box with his other possessions. He walked through with confidence, sure that he'd given them any metal object on his body. The alarm sounded again.

Everett dropped his shoulders. "Jesus Henry Christ," he groaned.

"Please step aside, sir."

Everett's worst fears about the airport became his nightmarish reality as a large bald man began to drag his hands along his body. He focused on Everett's sweat-coated armpits, then the waistband of his pants, working his way down to his ankles, and finally jamming his hands between Everett's legs.

"Oh my god, do you think I might have a bomb strapped to my taint?" Everett snapped.

"Please don't say bomb at the airport, sir," the man said as his hands more thoroughly checked Everett's nether regions.

Everett's jaw clenched as he looked at Maria, whose smile couldn't have been any wider.

"Clean," the man said.

Maria continued to chuckle as they jogged toward the gate.

"You mentioned a bomb at the airport. Have you lost your damn mind?" she said through her laughter.

"They acted like I was smuggling one in my asshole. I mean, really, has anyone tried to smuggle a bomb in their ass so far?"

"I'm sure people have tried."

"Besides, if I had a bomb up my ass, they wouldn't have found it with a pat down."

Nearby, people looked at Everett with a horrified stare.

"There's nothing in my ass," he said over his shoulder as they picked up their pace and rushed toward the gate. By the time they reached it, they'd almost missed the chance to board.

The flight attendant curled her lips at them. "Did you even read the time on the ticket?" She gestured toward the clock behind her, conveniently placed to shame them.

"We would have been on time, but your security guards tried to give me a rub and tug."

Maria stifled her laughter as the woman's face hardened. The attendant motioned toward the boarding bridge.

"Thank god," they both said as they sat down across the aisle from each other. Everett squeezed into the middle seat between two overweight passengers. Now there were three overweight passengers crammed in the row. Everett's arms squished together as the men on either side of him took up the armrests.

This is fine, everything is fine, he tried to tell himself as the plane began its ascent toward the sky.

A few hours into the flight, the man beside Everett snored and drooled as the lights flickered overhead. His body leaned and his head almost touched Everett's shoulder. The other man smacked his lips with every chip he shoveled into his waiting gullet. Whenever he laughed at the movie playing on the seat in front of him, a spray of spittle and greasy crumbs flew from his mouth.

Everett groaned and tried to imagine himself anywhere else. *If it weren't for Maria, I wouldn't have agreed to this trip.* His bladder throbbed until it made him feel sick. His urge to pee was undeniable, and his avoidance had come to an end. Unfortunately, the sleeping man beside him effectively blocked him in with his round gut. Everett gathered his courage and tapped on his shoulder, but he only snored louder in response.

"Sir!" Everett shouted. The man jumped, knocking into his tray and spilling his rum on Everett's pants. *Can this get any worse?* "I need to go to the bathroom."

The man grunted, struggling to stand as the armrest squeezed into his stomach. After wrangling his belly, he finally moved over for Everett, who accidentally pressed his ass against the man's crotch as he squeezed through.

These seats are dirty, I'm rubbing on everyone's body parts, and I smell like the floor of a bar. This is awful. Everett hurried toward the bathroom before any other tragedies could befall him.

"Sir." A petite blonde stewardess blocked him with her tiny arm, halting his beeline for the bathroom. She gestured toward the seatbelt sign. "You need to remain seated with your seatbelt fastened until that light goes off."

"Ma'am, I can either pee in the bathroom or in my seat. Your choice." He shifted his weight as his bladder screamed for relief.

She pursed her lips. "Fine."

Everett shuffled to the bathroom. He tried to open the door, but it was locked. *No, no, no.* Everett looked around at empty water bottles and glasses and tried to come up with an alternate plan. The bathroom door jiggled, and a short man apologized as he walked by. *No.* Everett closed his eyes before squeezing into the tiny room and struggling to close the door. A noxious odor filled his nose, singeing the hairs. He got his fly open just in time for the surge of urine to rush out of him in a fountain of relief.

The odor of the previous visitor seemed to grow stronger with every breath he took until he couldn't bear it any longer. He turned his head and vomited in the sink. Sudden turbulence—the reason for the seatbelt sign—made him lose his balance as he stared at his partially digested breakfast, and he dribbled pee on his pants.

"I'm going to fucking kill myself," Everett said under his breath as he dabbed his pants with toilet paper. Someone knocked on the door. "Hold on!" he yelled.

Renee appeared and stared at him with a harsh glare. "Why would you say that?" she asked before she looked around the murder scene that Everett had made of this bathroom. "Oh." She covered her mouth, hiding a hint of a smile.

"What do I even do?" Everett whispered, as if she had some otherworldly knowledge of how to get out of catastrophes. Technically, she did. She was a wife, and wives knew how to fix things. Anytime his vision grew foggy from anxiety and the panic obscured any chance of problem solving, Renee knew what to do.

"Use toilet paper to scoop it into the toilet," she said.

Everett groaned at the thought before he started furiously scooping wads of vomit out of the sink. He flushed everything before assessing the damage to his pants.

"Put a little soap and water on it," she said. "You'll be fine. Remember when I got pee on my dress at your grandma's funeral?"

He did as she directed, a frown growing on his face with every swipe of the toilet paper. "Now I just look like I pissed my pants. What am I even doing here, Renee? I don't like doing things."

"You're doing this for Maria. Try to relax and have a good time. I think you'll do better if I'm not hanging around, but no more threats of self-harm." She smirked before disappearing.

Everett walked out of the bathroom with a large dark spot on the front of his jeans. The stewardess looked at him and scrunched her nose.

"It's not pee," he snapped. "Well, not all of it is pee."

He hid his lap with his arms as he walked down the aisle. When he contorted his body into his seat, his neighbors gave him dirty looks. "I had something on my pants," he tried to tell them, but they didn't seem too convinced.

Everett tried to relax for the rest of his plane ride. He let his head drop to the side as his eyelids drooped, and he welcomed the idea of a nap. Just as his eyes began to close, a bare foot eased through the gap between the seats and grazed his arm. He stood and looked behind him. A middle-aged woman crocheted as fast as her fingers could go, oblivious to Everett's fiery gaze.

"Could you maybe not do that?" he said, motioning to her foot. "It's an armrest, not a footrest." He was half-sure he'd have a breakdown on the damn plane before they ever entered Vegas airspace. Maybe he'd be escorted off and he could avoid the trip altogether. Everett dropped back down with a huff. "Primitives," he mumbled.

He saw movement to his left, and he looked in time to see Maria doubled over with laughter as tears streamed from her eyes. *Glad one of us finds this funny.*

The plane finally landed, and Everett's knees shook with anxiety as he waited for every row in front of him to disembark. He dropped his head back with a sigh as passengers struggled to get their bags down, taking what felt like an eternity to get the fuck off the damn plane. When their row stood and removed their baggage from overhead, the large, sweaty man beside him reached up and shoved his armpits in Everett's face. He didn't even respond at that point. He just let the moist fabric rub on his cheek.

My life is a joke. It's official.

Everett hurried off the plane with the speed of a power walker after a large bump of coke.

"Everett! Wait up!" Maria shouted. She grabbed his arm and stopped his momentum. Gripping both of his arms, she stood in front of him. "Relax, we're here. It's fine. We'll ask at the desk if we can pay the upcharge and sit together on the ride back, okay? Don't let that plane ride ruin your time."

Everett stared at her as he put another piece of gum in his mouth. He didn't typically splurge for anything with an upcharge, but for this, he'd allow it. He nodded and felt the tight muscles in his neck begin to relax.

"Let's get to the hotel and get some liquor in you." Maria smiled and they exited the airport before Everett lost his shit.

CHAPTER TWENTY-FIVE

A s they approached the door to Everett's room, his heart rate still hadn't normalized. "I swear I'm not usually this uptight. That plane ride was just harsh," he said as he absentmindedly pulled his sheets from his suitcase, removed the hotel sheets, and started to remake the bed.

Maria's mouth dropped open. "Yeah . . . not uptight at all."

Everett stopped himself and looked down, finally seeing what she was seeing. "This? I always use my own sheets in hotels. Statistics show—"

"I don't care about statistics. Go ahead. Do your weird thing." She looked at her watch. "I'm going to the bar. Meet me down there?"

"I'll be right down."

Everett finished making the bed and changed into a polo shirt and a piss-free pair of pants. He tried not to think about Renee as he walked to the elevator, but it was difficult to avoid the pinprick of guilt in his stomach. She'd always wanted to go to Vegas, but he'd been too wrapped up in deadlines and defendants to make time to take her. Now here he was, seeing the city she always wanted to visit. Granted, this wasn't a vacation, but it didn't ease the regret he felt for never bringing her here.

The elevator opened into the lobby, and he made his way to the hotel bar. The sounds and lights from the slot machines overpowered his senses. It was no surprise people got drawn to them. They were hard as hell to ignore. Men and women sat at their machines, cranking the handle with emotionless faces like zombies at a carnival.

He spotted Maria sitting on a stool, swirling a drink in her hand. The seat beside her creaked as he sat down and stared at her. "Do you think I'm weird?" he asked.

"I already know you're weird." She slid a glass of bourbon toward him.

"I don't drink much hard liquor." Everett tried to pass it back to her.

"For the next two nights you do. Top-shelf drinks and they'll keep them coming for free." She smiled and wiggled her eyebrows.

Everett *did* love free stuff. He took a sip of the rich brown liquid as the ice cubes clinked against each other and chilled his lips. Before he'd finished the glass, the bartender brought him another at Maria's request.

"If I didn't know any better, I'd think you were trying to get me drunk to take advantage of me." He smirked.

She shrugged and turned to face him. "Maybe I am."

Everett's eyes wandered to the black fabric of her leggings. The liquor had given him some much-needed courage. He leaned closer and drew her toward him with a hand around the back of her neck. His lips met hers, and they kissed without reservation as if it were the most natural thing they'd done all day. Her hand moved to his leg, and she raked her nails along his thigh.

"Do you want another bourbon?" The bartender broke their kiss with the question.

Maria wiped her mouth and nodded. "Make it two."

After guzzling a few more drinks, Everett and Maria stumbled down the hall toward Everett's room. They laughed and hushed each other with their arms intertwined. As they hobbled down their hallway, a door opened beside them and McNinch walked out in swim trunks. Everett and Maria straightened their spines and tried to act sober, like two teenagers caught at the front door after sneaking out.

"Was it you two being so loud out here?" McNinch asked.

"No, there were some . . . kids . . . causing a ruckus." Maria stared at him with a smile. Everett saw her gaze drop over his chiseled abs, and he felt his stomach twist from jealousy. Or alcohol. Maybe both.

"I'm heading to the pool. Might get a workout in too," he said with lips moving just for Maria. "Want to meet me in the gym, Everett?"

Everett casually looked down at his belly in his polo shirt. *Absolutely not a chance in hell. Who works out at hotels?* Everett's eyes scanned McNinch's physique again. *Him, clearly.*

"No, I worked out earlier, so I'm going to have to pass. Next time, though, for sure."

Maria grinned and nudged Everett to keep walking with her. "Bye, Jeff," she called over her shoulder, stumbling a bit.

"First name basis?" Everett whispered, feeling another pang of jealousy.

"Oh, I just worried I might accidentally call him McBitch to his face instead of behind his back." She laughed. "Wouldn't be the first time."

Everett slid his keycard into the door multiple times before it finally clicked open with a flashing green light. They walked past the pile of discarded hotel linen.

"You even take off the comforter?" Maria asked with a tilt of her head.

"Have you seen the documentaries? If I had a black light, I could show you the bodily fluids all over it."

Maria rolled her eyes and flopped onto the bed. She let her knees fall to the side, accentuating her ass. Everett couldn't help but check her out. Again. He dropped onto the bed beside her and sighed.

"What time does the stupid conference start tomorrow?" he asked.

Maria grabbed her phone and scrolled through her emails. "Breakfast at seven, keynote speakers from eight to eleven, and boring-ass slideshows until two."

"Are the speakers any good?"

"They've worked the most high-profile cases of our lifetimes, so yeah."

Maria dropped her phone to the floor, leaned over, and kissed Everett. He tasted the acidic alcohol on her tongue. Her hands traced his chest, and she tried to lift his shirt. Everett stopped her and moved her hands away.

"Maria," he said, despite the protest of his dick. "I don't want to have sex with you when we're both this drunk. I would prefer to remember you. All of you." *Damn, I flirt well when I'm drunk.*

"Fine. I think I'll go get a quick workout in." She winked.

"Really?"

"No, I'm just kidding. I'm going to go to my room, turn on some trash television, and go to sleep. But if you change your mind, I'm in room 302." She leaned in and kissed him, leaving her room key on the TV stand on her way out the door.

Everett covered his face and groaned.

"Why the hell didn't you have sex with her? She was

laying it on so thick!" Renee said as she appeared on his bed. "Also, I see you're still bringing our sheets on trips."

"Renee, I'm not getting into this with you." Everett waved his hand dismissively and went into the bathroom. He unzipped his fly and started to pee. Renee continued speaking in the other room, but he couldn't hear her over his stream. "Dude, I can't even hear you. Hold on!" Everett tucked himself back into his boxers and started toward Renee, but she pointed her finger at the bathroom. With a roll of his eyes, he went back and flushed the toilet.

"I said I don't care if you have sex with Maria. I want you to be happy."

"I don't care that you don't care, because *I* care." Everett dropped onto the bed and closed his burning eyes. A light headache throbbed on the left side of his skull.

"What's holding you back?"

"You!" He thought for a moment. "And you said I was boring. It's really taken a shit on what little confidence I had to begin with."

Renee blinked at him. "I never said you were *boring*."

"Basically."

"You're insecure, and that's not a very attractive trait. If you're insecure, you aren't confident, and confident men can *fuck*."

Everett's temples throbbed from clenching his jaw. "Really? Is this supposed to make me feel better?"

"Yes, kind of. Indirectly. You were confident *tonight*. You were loose and you started to say some hot shit." Renee lifted an eyebrow. "You should have taken advantage of that."

Renee smiled as she lifted the skirt of her slip and exposed herself. Everett stared between her legs with a longing that he would never quite have for anyone else. Her fingers rubbed slowly up her thigh.

"Do they not have panties in the afterlife?" Everett looked away for a moment.

"They were optional," she said with a soft moan.

"Renee, we can't do this again," he said, although his dick screamed in defiance.

"Why not? I want you." Renee sat up.

"I need to move forward, and I can't do that if I keep going backward." He stood, opened the minibar, and downed more liquor. The bottles clanked as they fell to the table. He grabbed the key Maria left and headed out the door.

By the time Everett opened the door to Maria's room, the lights were off and only the TV illuminated the bed. Maria was fast asleep, her small frame somehow taking up the whole king-sized bed. The door slammed behind him and Everett cursed, but Maria didn't stir. With clumsy steps, he made his way to the bed. He stared at her soft curves before grabbing the comforter and tucking her in.

"Everett?" she said in a groggy voice.

"It's me."

She patted the bed. "Will you lay with me?"

He looked at her—and the possibly fluid-covered sheets—and froze. But it was time to move forward, even if it meant wallowing in someone else's dried semen. He sighed before moving the comforter back with one of his fingers as he crawled into the bed. Maria rolled over and draped her arm over his chest. Her breath brushed against his neck in a soothing rhythm, and he closed his eyes. His muscles relaxed and he fell asleep beside her.

CHAPTER TWENTY-SIX

E verett woke up with his arms wrapped around Maria. He looked at the alarm clock. *Shit.* "Maria." He shook her. "Maria, we overslept! It's six!"

She rolled onto her back, brushed the hair from her face, and groaned as she sat up. "Fuck. It's fine. We'll be fine."

They dragged themselves out of bed with a simultaneous grunt. Everett went to the sink and splashed cold water on his face to wake himself up. Maria opened her suitcase and pulled face wash and mascara from a pocket in the side.

"Did you know that stuff costs forty-five dollars?" Everett said as he patted a hand towel against his cheeks.

"*Pfft*, not for me. I won't pay more than ten dollars for this shit. It's just to avoid people telling me I look sick when I don't wear it."

Everett hurried to his room to dress in his suit. He smoothed the wrinkles the best he could and met Maria in the hotel lobby. She looked stunning. The hem of her skirt landed just short of her knees, putting all the attention on her perfect calves. She lit up when he entered the lobby, and she flashed a smile as he came toward her. They exited the hotel together and made their way to the rental car.

"Why did we need a convertible?" Everett asked as he sat in the very low sports car. "I'm practically on the ground."

She shrugged her shoulders. "Because why not? It's free!" She covered her eyes with her aviators and pulled out of the parking garage. Her dark, wavy hair blew in the breeze as they drove toward the conference center.

Everett found himself smiling as he put on his sunglasses. "Okay, I'll admit, this is kind of fun."

BY THE TIME the conference ended, Everett and Maria were dragging their feet out the front door. While it had been an enlightening day, it had also been a long—and sometimes boring—day. Maria made it more tolerable for him, though. They'd sat with each other throughout the event, making jokes and poking fun at the speakers and slides.

"I feel like a better lawyer already," Everett said with a grin.

Maria shook her head. "I don't. I'm pretty sure I don't want to be a lawyer anymore. Trying to nurse a hangover while listening to lawyers brag about their million-dollar successes was not a fun time."

"I didn't feel very hung over, yet I feel like I drank way more than you."

"I'm on medication for some mental health stuff, and drinking makes me real drunk real fast."

He smiled inwardly at the fact that, like him, Maria also struggled with her mental health. She was so put together and *normal*. It gave him hope for himself. They headed for the unnecessarily extravagant rental car and drove back toward the hotel.

They pulled into the parking garage and made their way to the hotel restaurant. Maria gave her name to the hostess, and they were brought to a table. The waiter brought them water, and Maria chugged it as if she'd just walked in from the desert.

"Thirsty?"

"Just a little. The alcohol dehydrated me. I think that's why I felt so hungover and shitty today."

Everett put his hand on hers and brushed his thumb over the back of her hand. "I'm sorry you feel sick."

"I feel . . . really—" She covered her mouth, leaped from the chair, and bolted toward the bathroom. By the time she returned, Everett had already explained things to the waitress and stood waiting for her outside the bathroom.

"What are you doing?" she asked, still pale and sick looking. "We don't need to leave."

"You're not well. Come on, let's go to my room." Everett let Maria lean on him as they walked toward the elevator and made their way down the hall.

Maria collapsed on his bed, and Everett wrapped her in a blanket before sitting beside her. He flipped on the TV and scanned the stations as she leaned over and put her head in his lap. *Don't get hard*, he commanded his dick. *Don't . . .*

"I feel that." Maria smirked.

"Sorry, it's . . . been a while." Everett looked down at the intricate pattern of the hotel carpet. He nearly lost his erection at the thought of just how unlikely it was that housekeeping did anything more than vacuum it. Ever.

Maria put her hand over her mouth, crawled out of bed, and ran to the bathroom.

He followed her and knocked on the bathroom door. "Do

you need me to hold your hair or something? I think that's what I'm supposed to offer."

"No, I need ginger ale. They probably have some in the hotel store. And crackers!"

He made his way to the lobby and found the small store tucked into the corner. Gaudy tourist shirts with kitschy sayings covered one wall. He made his way past them and scoured the cooler in the back for ginger ale. His jaw dropped at the pumped-up cost of a simple soda. *Criminal,* he thought as he grabbed it and some crackers and paid the inflated price at the counter.

Everett ran into McNinch in the hallway on his way back to his room. Thankfully, he was dressed this time.

"Hey, Everett, great conference, right?" His words slurred together, and his eyes were bloodshot and watery. "Are you in there with Maria?" He steadied himself against the wall. "I bet she's rocking your world, huh?"

Everett looked down at the ginger ale and crackers and shoved them behind his back.

"Yeah, so much . . . rocking," Everett said uncomfortably.

McNinch pointed at a colleague before stumbling away to greet them. He didn't even say goodbye to Everett, not that he particularly cared.

When he opened the door, he found Maria showered and in bed, wearing one of his t-shirts. He loved that damn look.

"I'm sorry," she said. "I hope you don't mind. I got puke on mine."

Everett didn't mind at all. Her body looked incredible in his shirt. It swallowed her, but it allowed her black panties to peek from beneath the hem. He shifted his weight as his excitement pitched a tent in the front of his pants. He reached down and tucked it into his waistband as he handed Maria the ginger ale and crackers.

"Did I hear McNinch yelling out there?" she asked. She screwed off the top of the soda and sipped it.

"Yeah. He's extremely intoxicated. He may or may not think you and I had sex. I'm sorry."

She nibbled the edge of a cracker. "Why?"

"He said you were probably 'rocking my world.' Out of curiosity, how much did you rock his world?"

"Oh my god, Everett. Please don't judge me for who I slept with, what? Six years ago? Yours is the only world I want to rock at this point. When you're ready." She took another sip of ginger ale.

"Soon . . ." he told her with uncertainty in his voice.

CHAPTER TWENTY-SEVEN

The flight home was much more anti-climactic. There was a screaming baby on board for the entirety of the flight, which gnawed at Everett's nerves, but having Maria right next to him made everything better.

"I'm sorry I had to wear your shirt. I'll get it back to you, fresh and clean," she whispered.

"Oh, no rush. I probably have four more shirts just like it."

"Of course you do." Maria laughed. "Sorry I got sick. I don't know what happened. I feel like I really missed an opportunity to seduce you."

"You totally did. I was just about to strip naked and pounce, but then you puked and ruined the moment."

She gave his arm a playful smack. "I'll make it up to you."

Mentally and physically exhausted, Everett drove home from the airport. His social meter was depleted, and he needed some alone time to recharge. The moment his body hit the couch cushion, Renee appeared beside him.

"Did you have fun? What was it like? Did you guys finally—"

"Renee, I'm tired."

"Stop being dramatic, you're fine."

Everett went to speak but the moment he opened his mouth, a rush of bile rose into his throat. He covered his mouth, ran to the bathroom, and vomited his breakfast, lunch, and airplane snacks into the toilet.

"Shit, I think Maria got me sick," Everett said as he leaned against the bathtub, sweat dripping down his forehead. He struggled to his feet and stumbled into the kitchen. "Renee, didn't we have some Gatorade?"

"I drank it at some point."

Everett groaned. "What? You're supposed to save it for sickness. The electrolytes."

"It's sugar water."

Everett wobbled back to the couch and lifted his phone. He dialed Maria. "I think whatever you had was contagious," he said when she answered. "I'm puking my guts up."

"No, I'm so sorry! Want me to come over?"

"Can you bring Gatorade?"

"Gatorade? Why?"

Am I the only person who drinks Gatorade because they're sick? "It'll make me feel better."

He curled into a miserable ball on the couch and waited for help to arrive. Renee stayed by his side, less to support him than to silently judge him. She always said he acted like the biggest baby when he was sick.

Maria showed up at his door within the hour with several flavors of Gatorade and a steaming bowl of chicken noodle soup. Everett smiled at her kind gesture and shivered under a blanket surrounded by tissues. He thanked Maria with a whine in his tone.

Renee rolled her eyes. "Stop being so pitiful. Did you see Maria acting like this?"

"Yes."

Maria cocked her head. "Huh?"

"Nothing, sorry. That looks really great." Everett took the warm Styrofoam bowl into his shaking hands and spooned some into his mouth. "I'm sorry, I think I'm too sick to rock your world now. Rain check?" His laugh was shaky, and he added extra dramatics with a cough.

"Oh, for fuck's sake," Renee said, throwing her hands in the air.

"I guess I'll have to accept it," Maria said as she pulled his head into her lap. She brushed her hand through his hair, which made his eyes heavy, so heavy, until he fell asleep.

WHEN EVERETT WOKE UP, Maria was curled up beside him, passed out. He watched her sleep. *Ew, why am I being a creep?* He didn't condone his behavior, but he couldn't help watching her lips part with every breath. Her chest rose and fell rhythmically. Everett covered his lap with his arm. *Guess my dick isn't sick.*

She stirred awake and looked him up and down. "How are you feeling?"

"Better, I think." Everett smiled as he wrapped his arms around her and pulled her into him. He nuzzled into her warm neck and kissed the soft skin of her shoulder.

She tilted her head away from him. "Don't start something you can't finish, Everett," she said with a playful laugh.

"Fine." He nibbled on her neck one final time before looking around the room. Renee had vanished while they slept. He'd seen less and less of her lately, and she'd hardly appeared at all during his business trip. It bothered him to think about how much time she spent in that white room.

What if I really am the reason Renee is still here? How hard had he tried to move on? Not hard enough. The incredible woman in his arms had offered herself to him and as much as he liked her, he still hadn't been able to seal the deal. He needed help to move past his roadblocks and insecurities. If he felt better tomorrow, he'd suck it up and see a shrink.

CHAPTER TWENTY-EIGHT

E verett was trapped in a pit of despair. He dropped his head back and sighed as he wet his hair and parted it down the side. After sliding a pair of sunglasses over his tired eyes, he grabbed his keys and went to his car. Against his better judgment, he was on his way to see a therapist, finally ready to admit to himself that he struggled to move on as much as Renee. All the pieces of his happiness puzzle had fallen into place, yet he was still miserable. He'd secured the job he'd wanted for several years, and he was dating the number one defense attorney in the area, but here he was, still thinking about his dead wife.

Everett opened the door to the therapist's office with very little hope of achieving anything from it. The young secretary looked up and smiled.

"Name?" she said as she adjusted her glasses.

"Ever . . . ton. Everton Smith."

"Okay, Everton, have a seat. You'll be called in shortly."

She returned her attention to her cell phone as Everett looked around the waiting room. He wanted a seat that wasn't near anyone else, but with the number of people in the waiting room, it didn't look possible. At least depression wasn't contagious. He chose a seat against the wall so he'd only have someone to his right, and there was still a chair between them. He didn't take off his dark sunglasses. The thought of someone recognizing him made his skin crawl.

Everett looked at his watch and groaned. If he left now, he could still beat lunch-hour traffic and make it home in time to watch the showcase contestants on *The Price Is Right*. He got to his feet and started for the door, but someone called his fake name just as his hand curled around the silver door handle.

"Everton Smith?"

He turned and saw a balding man in the doorway on the other side of the room. He clutched a manila folder to his chest and offered Everett a kind smile through his white beard. Though his feet wanted to keep moving toward his car, Everett followed the man down a beige hallway and into a room. The man turned on a white noise machine just past the doorway in his office.

"What's that for?" Everett asked.

"Privacy. Have a seat." The man gestured toward the lumpy couch in front of him and planted himself in a large leather chair, his dangling feet unable to reach the ground. "Are you going to take off your sunglasses, Everton?"

"No," Everett said. He looked around the small, informal office. He expected certifications and diplomas to line the walls, but the credentials were absent. *I thought they had to hang those up. This guy could be anyone.*

"Alright. On your paperwork you wrote that you're still struggling with the loss of your wife. Can you tell me more about that?"

"My wife is dead and I'm struggling with it," Everett said in a flat voice.

Renee appeared beside him and looked around with wide

eyes. "What is even happening right now?" She gestured toward Everett's disguise and laughed.

"Shh," Everett shushed her.

"Sorry?" The therapist looked at him like he had fourteen heads.

Everett had messed up and spoken to Renee in front of a therapist, of all people. He'd have to elaborate on his answer to get the attention away from his misstep. "I'm struggling with the loss of my wife because I feel like our marriage wasn't what I thought it was."

"In what ways?" The therapist rubbed his beard, picked up his pencil, and scribbled something in the folder.

"I thought she was happier than she was. I thought *I* was happier than I was."

"I want you to talk as if you're talking to your wife. I'm hearing a lot of guilt, so it could help to say these things to her."

Renee released an annoyed sigh. "I told you seventeen times that I *was* happy. I *am* happy."

"Happy people don't kill themselves for no reason, Renee."

"Good, good," the therapist said. He sat forward in his seat, clearly enthralled by Everett's willingness to participate in the exercise. If he only knew.

"Something caused me to take my own life," Renee continued, "but it was for you."

"For me?" Everett sat up straight and raised his voice at Renee as she sat on the cushion beside him—the cushion that would appear empty to the therapist. "I did everything for you, Renee. I bought you everything you wanted, and I would have done anything you asked."

"Except come home a few nights a week so we could have dinner together or have sex with me more than once a month."

"You were lonely, I get it, but I don't know what you wanted me to do. I couldn't just abandon my job. You wanted bamboo sheets and forty-five-dollar mascara. I couldn't provide that shit at an average nine-to-five." Everett shrugged and lifted his hands in exasperation. "It's not like you were working."

The therapist's eyes grew wide, and his lips formed a straight line. He dropped his pencil and stared at Everett.

"Are you fucking kidding me? *You* told me to give up my bartending job. I had no problem serving drinks." Renee stood up and Everett's eyes followed her as she paced the room.

"Excuse the fuck out of me for wanting to prevent other men from sexually assaulting my wife in their perverted minds every night."

"You're missing the point, Everett! You aren't the reason I slit my fucking wrists!"

"You remember why you killed yourself, don't you?" He glared at her through the dark lenses of his sunglasses. She couldn't say why she *hadn't* killed herself unless she also knew why she *had*.

"I don't remember," she whispered, her gaze dropping to the floor.

The therapist opened his mouth to speak, but Everett held out his hand, silencing him while keeping his eyes on Renee.

"The fuck you don't. You said you did it for me. How do you know that if you don't know why you did it?" Everett raised his voice and got to his feet. "Stop lying to me, Renee! Tell me the truth!"

She stopped pacing and turned to face him, her eyes filled with tears. "I fucking had an affair, Everett!" She dropped to her knees and buried her face in her hands. "I had an affair."

Everett's jaw dropped, and he fell backward onto the

couch. The walls closed in on him and a vise gripped his stomach, twisting and squeezing until he felt as if he would be sick. He looked around for a garbage can. His lungs forgot the motions they'd performed his entire life, while his heart doubled its speed. His eyebrows pulled together and the world seemed to fade.

No . . . the world wasn't fading. *Renee* was fading. He rubbed his eyes and looked again, but it wasn't a trick brought on by his panic. He could see through her.

Everett hadn't been the one holding her back all this time. The secret she took to the grave had tethered her to this world—a heavy chain coiled around her waist, securing her in place. But she hadn't revealed enough. There was more to her secret.

"Who was it, Renee? Please tell me you didn't fuck Clarke. He made a comment—"

"Gross," she said through sobs. "I'd rather masturbate with a broken bottle than go anywhere near him." She lifted her head and looked him in the eyes. "It's worse, Everett, and I'm sorry it ever happened. I never wanted you to know."

"Who was it?"

Too many seconds passed between them. Muffled words came from the therapist in front of him, but his focus was solely on Renee and her confession.

He shook his head. "I don't care who it was. We could have worked through this. You didn't need to—"

"Roman," Renee whispered.

Everett's chest tightened, and for a moment he wondered if all his takeout was actually taking *him* out right now. The pain in his chest cut off his breath. Was it a heart attack or his heart breaking? "Roman?" he asked. "Like, my brother Roman? *That* Roman?"

"I'm so sorry . . ." Renee shimmered, and a light glow grew around her frame.

His lips quivered. He didn't want to hear anymore, didn't want to know another detail. Each layer of her confession drove a fresh dagger into his chest. But he had to hear it. It was the only way she could finally find her peace. "How long?"

"It wasn't very long. A few months, maybe. He wanted to tell you, and I couldn't bear the thought of you finding out. I didn't think he'd tell you if I took out the trash for you."

Everett gritted his teeth. Despite how much he hurt, he couldn't put all the blame on her. "You aren't trash. It's my fault too. I wasn't around enough, and I didn't give you what you needed. The sheets and makeup and expensive things couldn't fill the empty chair across from you at the dinner table. They couldn't fill the empty place in your heart."

The light around her grew until it almost obscured her faint image.

"I loved you, Renee Enders. I will always love you. And I forgive you."

Her mouth moved, but he could no longer hear her voice as she disappeared, the light fading with her. He covered his mouth and wept, nearly collapsing as his legs shook beneath him.

"Great roleplaying," the therapist said. His papers and the pen lay on the table beside him, forgotten as he witnessed what he believed to be a man working through a problem.

But it was more than that. He'd witnessed a man saying goodbye for the last time.

EVERETT PULLED into the familiar driveway in the familiar neighborhood and got out of the car, slamming the door behind him. Even his footsteps sounded angry as he marched toward the front door. He'd had the whole car ride to think about what he wanted to say, yet he still didn't know what might come out of his mouth.

Everett raised his fist and beat against the door. When it didn't open, he walked to the garage and peered through the window. The sports car was there, which meant his brother had to be inside. He walked back to the door and pounded harder until it finally swung open. Roman stood before him in his boxers, wiping his eyes.

"What are you doing here?" He stepped aside to let Everett in. "Is everything okay, bro?"

Everett stepped into his brother's quaint home. "No, everything is *not* okay." He drew his arm back and punched Roman in the nose. It knocked his brother off balance and sent him stumbling backward against the island in the kitchen. Roman righted himself and wiped blood away from his nostrils.

"What the fuck was that for? Have you lost your mind?" Blood dripped past Roman's lips, and he spat it onto the floor.

"You fucked my wife!" Everett yelled as he charged forward. He knocked his brother to the ground and straddled him, sending a message through his fists as he throttled his face. "You piece of shit!"

"Who told you?" Roman wailed through the assault.

"She did!" Everett gave him one more solid punch before climbing off with heavy breaths. "She told me everything!"

Roman got to his knees as blood fell in a scarlet veil over his face.

"How?" The word splattered blood on the floor below him.

"I tried to tell you I could talk to Renee. Her spirit was haunting me, *bro*." He mocked his brother's endearing term

215

for him. "She was stuck here because of your happy little affair."

Roman pulled himself to his feet and put his hands up in a show of defeat. "I'm sorry, Everett."

"*Sorry?* Fuck you! You fucked the only person that mattered to me! You had everything you ever wanted, but you couldn't let me have one fucking thing for myself!" Everett tried to regain his breath, the fight being the most exercise he'd had in a while. "*You* are the reason she's gone!"

"No, Everett, don't. I didn't take her life. She came onto *me*, not the other way around."

"Do *not* blame her," Everett said through clenched teeth. "You played your fucking part in this. That night at my house . . . you knew her favorite dish because you took her to Ralph's. The place that meant something to us. You played your fucking part, now own it!"

Roman's hands fluttered in front of him. "I shouldn't have let it go farther than that, but I did, and I'm sorry!"

"I could understand fucking up one time, but you were having an affair for a while. You looked me in the eyes so many times while knowing you fucked my wife. You then continued to fuck my wife. What kind of sick person can do that? And you didn't think to tell me after she died?"

"Who am I to tell you that your wife had an affair? What's the point?"

"Because you are my fucking brother, Roman!" Tears welled in Everett's eyes. "This is like, the third woman you've taken from me. Are you jealous? What is it? Why can't *I* have someone nice without you putting your dick in her?"

Roman ran his hand through his hair. "I don't have an education or a big successful lawyer career, and I'm not as smart as you. Am I a little jealous?" He laughed without humor. "Yeah, maybe. You can give these women what I can't, which is a future. But I can give them something you can't. Passion."

Everett's eyes squinted and his jaw tightened. He wanted to punch him again, right in the mouth, but his arms were tired and he was still out of breath. An uncomfortable truth hung in the air between them. *I'm not passionate, and I don't know how to please women like Roman or Clarke. I'm not some horny freak who can't look past the junction between a woman's legs. I am a lover. I am just me.*

Everett rubbed his temples. "You're a piece of shit. We're done." He walked out the door, slamming it as he left.

CHAPTER TWENTY-NINE

The sound of Maria's familiar heels came up behind Everett. He looked back at her with a smile as she stepped closer and sat in the chair beside him.

"You didn't have to leave work to come here," he whispered.

She put her hand over his. "Yes, I did. This is more important than some murder case."

"It's not, but okay," Everett said, turning his attention back to the man standing at the podium. A smile hovered on his face at her willingness to carve out time for him, especially when the setting was a rinky-dink church with stale cookies and depressing stories.

Maria crossed her legs as she listened to the speaker.

The man with the yacht continued with his story yet again. He whimpered and blew his nose into a tissue. "I know she wouldn't want me to sell the boat. She loved that boat."

This time, Everett saw how the man kept his wife's memory alive by sharing stories with this room of strangers. His hands shook as he talked about the garden where she'd failed to grow anything more than weeds. The bird houses he made for her that she hung in the dogwoods in front of their house. The way she sometimes snorted when she had a good laugh. By the time he walked back to his chair, Maria had mascara running down her face as tears rolled down her cheeks. Everett choked back a tear of his own.

The group leader stood before the group and clapped his hands together. "That's all for to—"

"Is there time for one more?" Everett asked, lifting his hand in the air.

The group leader fumbled for words. It probably wasn't often that someone requested they stay later than usual. "Y-yes, I think that would be okay." He motioned toward the podium and went back to his seat.

Maria stared at Everett and lifted her eyebrow as he stood and walked to the front of the group. A trail of murmurs followed him with each step he took down the aisle. He leaned into the microphone and cleared his throat.

"Hi, I'm Everett Enders. Some of you might remember me as the guy who wouldn't participate, ate a bunch of cookies, and let a cat out of the building." He chuckled awkwardly and was surprised to hear a few gentle laughs in the crowd. "I want to take a moment to apologize for my previous visit and tell you a little more about my loss. Last time, I wasn't quite ready to share, but I'm ready now. I think."

He placed his hands on the podium and took a deep breath. "I found my wife after she committed suicide back in April. She was the most important thing in my life and the greatest loss I've ever experienced. And that's saying a lot because I was a defense attorney until just recently." He winked at Maria, and she gave him a smile that encouraged him to keep going. "I had the rare opportunity to really analyze and learn more about my wife and my marriage after she passed away, and while it was difficult, it made me a better person. *She* made me a better person. She reminded me how much I loved her and how I sometimes wanted to wring her neck as well." Everett laughed, and so did some of the crowd. "Last week, I learned what pushed her to take her life. Many people aren't this lucky. Some people walk every step with the weight of the unknown on their shoulders after losing someone to suicide. Not knowing drove me to depression, drinking . . . and too much take out." He patted his belly. "Learning the truth didn't make me feel much better, but it allowed me to grieve and begin to move forward with my life."

He paused and cleared his throat again, trying to dislodge the lump growing behind his Adam's apple. "If she were still alive, I know she'd be in the crowd with her jaw on the floor at the sight of me talking about my *feelings* in front of strangers. But this was important to me. You guys are stronger than I was able to be, and I thank you for giving me the chance to get back up here today." He smiled as he fought back a rogue tear threatening to fall down his cheek. He looked toward the back of the room, expecting to see Renee rolling her eyes and shaking her head.

But she wasn't there.

The crowd rose to their feet and applauded as Everett returned to his seat. Maria stood and embraced him in a strong, comforting hug.

"See, this *was* more important," she whispered in his ear.

CHAPTER THIRTY

M aria's hands trailed down Everett's body, and he shivered at her gentle touch. They collapsed in his bed, their jackets stripped off at the door. Her hands worked the buttons of his dress shirt, unfastening them until his chest was exposed. Her fingers grazed his skin, and her nails sent another shiver up his spine as they crept toward the waistband of his pants.

He placed a gentle hand over hers, stopping her. "Maria," he groaned before grabbing her face and drawing her toward him.

"You always stop us. Why? Is there something wrong with me?" Maria looked up at him with her eyebrows pulled together.

"No, there is absolutely nothing wrong with you. You are . . ." He shook his head. "Incredible. You're beautiful and smart and terrifying."

She slapped his chest and laughed. "Terrifying?"

"I'd never want to be pitted against you in court, that's for sure."

"I'm confident, not terrifying."

"I know, but I need to be honest with you. At first I stopped us because I still struggled with letting go of Renee. But I'm also nervous about . . . other things."

Maria sat up with a terrified glaze to her brown eyes. "Oh, fuck. You don't have herpes or something, do you?"

Everett laughed and pulled her back down. "No, I'm not harboring any diseases." He cleared his throat, terrified to speak his insecurities out loud. "I struggle with my appearance. I didn't even want to take my shirt off with Renee." Everett looked down at the thin layer of dark, curly hair covering his pale chest. The shirt was still buttoned over his stomach—the fiery source of his insecurity. "I also got some feedback that my bedroom skills may be lacking in some areas." He furrowed his brow and waited for her to run for the door. He expected her to be put off by his honesty.

But she wasn't.

She snuggled closer to him and laid her head on his chest. "Well, I like how you look, and regarding the other matter, I imagine it's a lack of experience versus a lack of skill. Most women have trouble teaching a man how to fuck them." She lifted her head and looked into his eyes. "But I'm not most women." She lifted her skirt and straddled his waist. Her black panties rode up her hips, exposing more of her ass as she ripped his shirt apart, sending the buttons flying across the room.

That was a new shirt! he thought as she pulled the fabric away and tossed it to the floor. His worry disappeared when she didn't run and hide at the sight of his doughy stomach. Anxiety bubbled to the surface the lower her hands trailed, but his dick still rose to meet the heat between her legs.

Maria started to unbutton her dress shirt, but Everett pushed her hands away and tried to rip it open as she had ripped his. He struggled a bit before the buttons popped off and skittered across the floor. He leaned up to slip the remains of her shirt down her arms.

Oh god. His mouth watered at the sight of her cleavage beneath a black bra, her breasts pulled close together in an intoxicating crease of flesh. He cupped them with his hands and squeezed. Her nipples pressed against the lace.

Everett rolled her onto her back and crawled between her legs. He worked off his pants and stopped with a purse of his lips. "Don't be mad, but I have to fold these because I still don't know how to iron without catching my house on fire." He smiled uncomfortably as he stood.

"Well, here. You might as well fold this too." She lifted her hips and squirmed out of her skirt.

Everett folded their garments and placed them on the dresser before crawling between her legs again and finding her mouth in a single motion. He wrapped a hand around the back of her neck and kissed her with a passion he didn't expect from himself. Their lips moved together as their bodies pressed closer. As a soft moan whispered from Maria's mouth, the throb of his dick became nearly unbearable.

He reached his hand between her legs and rubbed her through her silky black panties. The warm, wet heat encouraged his fingers to explore. Sitting up on his knees, he grabbed the waistband of her panties and slid them down her thighs until she could kick them off. She worked off her bra and tossed it aside. Her breasts spread and relaxed, but they were still perfect. He rubbed himself for a moment before pulling down his boxers and pressing himself against her.

"Are we doing this right now?" he whispered.

"Why are you so weird?" She laughed and wiggled her hips to grind against him.

Everett hesitated for a moment, worried Renee would pop up and scold him for what he was about to do. Naked flesh to naked flesh. When the room stayed silent and they remained alone, he pushed inside her with a groan.

Everett's thrusts were calm and controlled, not rough or fast. He was who he was.

"Harder," Maria said through a moan.

Ask and you shall receive. He shed his insecurities and fears and thrust into her, moving harder and faster as her body responded to him. He leaned closer and her breasts brushed against his chest as her moans grew louder. She wrapped her arms around him, raking his back with her nails.

Think of something else, anything else, but don't come yet! he shouted in his mind. He needed to please her, and coming after a thirty-second fuck wouldn't accomplish that. Anxiety flooded his mind, washing over him like a wave, and he pulled out.

"What are you—"

Everett dropped between her legs.

"Oh." She grabbed a fistful of his hair as his mouth caressed her.

His tongue found the spots that made her tense and arch her back as he tasted her. He listened to the way she breathed and moaned, using it as a roadmap to guide her closer to the edge. She gripped his hair tighter, pulling him closer. He couldn't breathe, but he didn't care. He wanted her to come. She rocked her hips against his mouth, and her thighs shook on either side of his head. She cried out his name as she came—his name—and it was all he needed. The tide of insecurity and anxiety receded as the wave of her orgasm rose.

At that moment, as she was weak from the surge of pleasure rippling through her body, he spread her thighs and pushed inside her again. Each satisfied whimper that slipped from her parted lips brought him closer.

"Can I come?" he whispered, barely able to get the words

out over his rising orgasm. Only after her quick nod did he let himself finish. He moaned against her neck and fell beside her, his chest rising and falling as if he'd run a marathon. "Fuck." Everett dropped his head back and groaned.

Maria curled into him, still sweaty and wet, and nuzzled into his chest. She looked up at him and bit her lip. "Your skills . . . are just fine."

Everett smiled and kissed her. He'd gotten the job and he'd gotten the girl, but it took Renee finding peace to truly reach his happy ending.

After all, happy wife, happy life.

EPILOGUE

Renee stood in the white room and stared at the wooden door that had appeared when she found herself transported back after Everett's therapy session. Technically, it had been her therapy session too. She'd gotten a lot off her chest, and that's what made her so afraid to open the door.

Where did it all go wrong? she thought as she stared at the brass knob. *I was happy. I was fine.* Until she wasn't. Then she'd cheated on her husband with his brother—a double betrayal. Guilt consumed her after that first tryst, but she hadn't stopped. She'd met him in public, going to dinner with him at a place that meant something to her and her husband. She'd watered down her guilt by telling herself it was okay because Everett didn't have time for her anymore, and she *needed* time. She needed to feel wanted again.

So why didn't I just tell him that? Why did I put my husband's heart at risk?

An affair was a slippery slope, and before Renee realized what was happening, she'd aimed her sled right at a tree. She recalled the exact text that put her over the edge and made her choices so unbearable that she had to end her life. That single message that made her decision for her. She was fine until her phone chimed on April 24.

Hey, I know you told me you don't want to tell him, but Everett deserves to know. I didn't know I'd fall in love with you when we started this, but I have. If you don't tell him tonight, I'll tell him tomorrow. I want to be with you, and I can't live like this. I have no problem telling him, but I think it will sound better coming from you. I love you, and I'm sorry it has to be this way. I just can't sneak around anymore. I hope you understand.

The message made her stomach sink and her heart break. Her options were to break the heart of the man she loved or to end her life before her lover could confess their secret. If she killed herself, Roman wouldn't tell Everett anything. Who would tell the man who just lost his wife that he'd been fucking her on the side? After the text, ending her life had been the only answer that made sense. Everett didn't deserve the pain the truth would cause, and Renee didn't feel she deserved to live.

Besides, the nagging suicidal thoughts had plagued her since she was a teen. A concoction of antidepressants and anti-anxiety meds gave her some semblance of normalcy in her head, but she'd always been one crisis away from hurling herself over the edge.

Renee drew her attention back to the door, shuddering at the memories of her past transgressions. She'd tried to make Everett's life better to make up for it, but would it be enough? What waited for her on the other side of that door? With a deep breath, she gripped the knob and stepped across the threshold—into light.

CONNECT WITH LAUREN

Check out LaurenBiel.com to sign up for the newsletter and get VIP (free and first) access to Lauren's spicy novellas and other bonus content!

Join the group on Facebook to connect with other fans and to discuss the books with the author. Visit http://www.face book.com/groups/laurenbieltraumances for more!

Lauren is now on Patreon! Get access to even more content and sneak peeks at upcoming novels. Check it out at www. patreon.com/LaurenBielAuthor to learn more!

ACKNOWLEDGMENTS

Thank you to my hubs, who continues to support (and annoy me) from this life. I love you!

Thank you to my editor, who helped me work through a story that was so different from my usual stuff. She had to pivot full circle to help me make this the story it became.

A special shout-out to my family, who is probably the reason I use dark humor as a coping mechanism.

ALSO BY LAUREN BIEL

Novels

Shoot Down the Stars

Colliding Stars

The Room to the West

Never Let Go

Novellas

Toxic Love

Toxic Desires

Men of Mayhem

Men of Vengeance

Wanted

ABOUT THE AUTHOR

Lauren Biel is an author with several titles in the works. When she's not working, she's writing. When she's not writing, she's spending time with her husband, her friends, or her pets. You might also find her on a horseback trail ride or sitting beside a waterfall in Upstate New York. When reading her work, expect the unexpected.

To be the first to know about her upcoming titles, please visit www.LaurenBiel.com.